Escape from Exile

Robert Levy

Houghton Mifflin Company
Boston

Library of Congress Cataloging-in-Publication Data

Levy, Robert, 1945–
    Escape from exile / Robert Levy.
        p.   cm.
    Summary: Thirteen-year-old Daniel is transported to the land of
Lithia, where he discovers that his ability to communicate mentally
with the strange native animals makes him a key figure in that country's
civil war.
    ISBN 0-395-64379-1
    [1. Fantasy.]   I. Title.
PZ7.L5836Es 1993   92–20443
[Fic]—dc20   CIP
                           AC

Printed in the United States of America

BP   10   9   8   7   6   5   4

For Ilsa, who is not only my wife, but my best friend.

Thank you for being there.

Prologue

On a deserted mountain, more than a hundred miles from the nearest village, forty-one elders sat in a large circle. It was just after dawn, when the twin moons had sunk in the west and the sun had just poked its head up in the east. Fog began to form as the first hints of warmth touched the cold night air. In the center of the circle sat the oldest elder, the leader of all the clans.

"I have called you here to talk about our future," he said. "We are dying. Each year, there are fewer of us born, and it is harder to find food. We must do something."

"Some of our young wish to fight," said one voice. "If they are going to die, they want to die fighting."

"We cannot win such a war," said the voice from the center of the circle. "We are outnumbered, thousands to one."

"We could move again," said another voice. "If we cross the mountains, we will find other lands to live on."

"Our enemy is like the sea, endless. They will be there, too," said the old voice from the center.

"You are telling us that we cannot stay where we are and we cannot move to another place."

"Yes," answered the voice.

"Then you are telling us nothing to bring back to our clans. We risk our lives meeting here. Was that risk taken only to hear what we already know?" said the voice of the youngest elder.

"No," answered the one in the center. "You are here to attend a mind-send. You are here so we can send our thoughts and our power into the great beyond, to the One-Who-Watches. We are prisoners in our clan sites. We must ask the One-Who-Watches for help. If we, as a race, are to survive, we must find a way of making peace with our enemies. We must find a way to speak to them. Come to me, my brothers. As the sun rises, so will our call for help."

"And how will that help come?" asked the youngest elder again.

"If I knew that, I would be the One-Who-Watches, and our people's lives would not be so hard. Join with me and let us send our power into the heavens."

The forty elders walked toward their leader until they were touching each other. Then the old one in the center, the one with a scar on his shoulder, looked up into the brightening sky. "Now," he said. "Now."

Chapter 1

"Daniel, use your head. Your sister is safe! You just spoke to her on the phone. You can't go home, you just can't. There are six inches of snow on the ground already, and it's coming down faster than ever."

Daniel Taylor got up and walked around the desk of Mr. Howard, the principal of his junior high school. He stopped by the window and stared at the blowing snow. He couldn't even see the tree that grew fifteen feet beyond the glass.

"You remember my sister, don't you?"

Mr. Howard leaned back in his cushy leather chair. "I'll never forget Evelyn. No one in this school will. She was the brightest student we ever had. She was also the youngest. How old was she when she started the seventh grade?"

"Eight. She graduated when she was nine. That was two years ago and she's graduating high school in June."

3

"So what are you worried about? Evelyn's a certified genius, a child prodigy. She'll be fine by herself."

"Mr. Howard, what kind of girl is Evelyn?" asked Daniel, turning around.

"It's been a long time since she was here. I'm not sure I can answer that." Daniel shook his head as he looked up at the ceiling. "All right," said Mr. Howard. "She was a brat. She was spoiled, threw tantrums when she didn't get her way, and never let anyone, especially her teachers, forget how bright she was."

"That's Evelyn, the eleven-year-old genius without any friends. No one who doesn't *have* to put up with her does. My parents are great people, but they're so wrapped up in their careers that they don't spend very much time with us; I've been a latch-key kid since I was eight. Evelyn doesn't have anyone else except me. Look, Mr. Howard, I know she's a pain who takes my stuff, embarrasses me when I'm with my friends, and has the ability to make my life miserable. But she's my sister and deep down—we're talking real deep now—I love her. She may have the I.Q. of a genius, but she's still a little girl who's afraid of the dark, afraid of thunder, and afraid of being home alone."

"But Daniel, she *is* safe. She's home and it's not thundering outside. If you want to, you can stay in my office and keep her on the phone until we can get you home safely."

"There's no way Mom and Dad can possibly get home from Philly today. They might be stuck there for three days, and if I don't leave now, I might even have

4

to spend the night here. Mr. Howard, if you won't think of Evelyn, at least think of me."

"I don't understand," said the principal.

"We agree my sister's not normal. I have a cat. That's a normal pet, no big deal. Sis, on the other hand, has to be different. She has four pet snakes."

"What's your point, Daniel?"

"I'm afraid of snakes, Mr. Howard, and Evelyn likes to take them out of their tanks and play with them. The three-foot boa is okay because he's big and I can see him. But the garter snakes . . . the garter snakes are small and fast, and when they get out of her room it takes us forever to find them. Sometimes, the brat takes them out and hides them! Do you know what it's like to take out a pair of underpants and find a sleeping snake curled up inside it? I do! Not once, but three times!" said Daniel, holding up three fingers. "Do you know I never get dressed in the morning without going into her room and counting snake heads? Do you know what fiendish plots of revenge a genius eleven-year-old can think of because I let a little snow keep me from getting home? I'm sorry, Mr. Howard, but I have to go. I'll be fine. I only live two miles from here, and if I cut through Foster Woods, it's less than a mile."

Daniel walked away from the window and picked up his coat.

"I won't force you to stay," said Mr. Howard. "But promise you'll call me as soon as you're home."

Daniel just nodded as he zipped up his parka and tied the hood cord around his neck. Ten minutes later he entered Foster Woods. Twenty minutes later he was hopelessly lost. The wind was raging, fighting him for every step. Flakes of soft snow were now spears of hard crystal, each one aimed directly at him. Even the leafless trees offered no protection from the wind. The short cut he took before the fury of the blizzard charged down on him was now the longest trail he had ever traveled.

He could no longer face the wind, so he turned and walked where it pushed. It forced him to run next to an old, leafless hedge. He tried to slow up, but the wind wouldn't let him. Branches whipped across his face, tearing at his frozen skin. Warm blood froze when it leaked through the scratches. His chest had begun to ache when something buried deep under the white blanket grabbed his feet. He stumbled and fell into a small hole hidden in the snow.

Daniel was afraid, really afraid. The cold was numbing, and he knew he had no strength left to fight the wind. He pulled his knees up to his head, making himself into a tight ball. But it was difficult because the hole wasn't big enough for his thirteen-year-old body, and he shivered violently. His eyes started to close and his mind began to wander. He imagined himself sitting by the fire in his own living room, drinking a cup of hot chocolate. He heard his mother in the kitchen; he saw his father reading the paper on the dining-room table. He even felt his sister when she sat down next to him, and they stared together at the crackling fire.

Suddenly, a loud thunderclap shook the air above his head. Daniel opened his eyes and looked up just as a lightning bolt in the shape of a perfect Z hit the ground several feet away from him. The pleasant daydream Daniel was having shattered as he remembered where he was. He brushed the snow off his head as he began to get up. A second clap of thunder rang out. "Thunder doesn't happen in blizzards," he said to himself. "Thunder! Oh no, I've got to get home. Evelyn!" Just as he spoke, a second bolt of Z-shaped lightning exploded inches above his head, throwing him back down and into a deep, unwanted sleep.

When Daniel opened his eyes, he felt dry, hard ground beneath him. He stretched and yawned, letting the sun warm his cheeks as he sat up. He felt refreshed. "Wait a minute," he said to himself. "Where am I? Something's wrong." Quickly, he looked around. "This isn't right! This isn't Foster Woods. Where's all the snow?" He found himself sitting on a gently sloping hill with emerald-green grass growing under him. Reaching to the sky, huge trees grew all around him. "Those trees are bigger than redwoods," he said, as he leaned back, scratching his head and staring straight up. "Trees like this don't grow in Pennsylvania." When he looked back down, he noticed his clothes. Instead of his own, he was wearing charcoal-gray pants and a chocolate-brown shirt, both made of a coarse leatherlike material. "How did I get these?" he wondered aloud. "They're not mine." He put his right hand on his left arm and squeezed. Feeling his own pinch made him feel a little better because he knew he was neither dead nor dreaming. "If

I didn't know better, I'd say Evelyn was playing tricks with my brain. But even she's not that smart."

He got up and searched the area, hoping to find something that might tell him where he was. The only thing he saw was the flattened grass where he lay. "Hello!" he shouted. But all he heard was a faint echo of his own voice as it bounced from tree to tree. He started walking up the hill and was soon threading his way among the monstrous trees. Wherever he was, it was early morning, because the sun had just begun its long climb to the center of the sky. As he walked deeper into the trees, he was bathed in shadows. The many leaves above him grabbed what sun they could, leaving little light to fall on the forest floor.

He walked faster, hoping that there was something else besides trees alive in these woods. But the only sounds he heard were his own footsteps, the only things he saw were the gigantic trees. He wished he knew where he was or how he got there. The last thing he remembered before waking up was the odd-shaped lightning exploding over him. He thought of many questions as he walked, but no one was there to supply him with answers.

The sun was at his left, so he knew he was heading south. That direction was as good as any. Eventually, he hoped, he would meet someone. Suddenly, as he continued walking deeper into nowhere, he heard a buzzing noise in his head. He waved his hands near his ears, hoping to shoo away some insect. But the buzzing didn't go away. Then a dull, throbbing ache began in his right hand. He turned, facing the morning sun. The buzzing became louder, the ache a little sharper.

"Hello!" shouted Daniel again, as he ran in that direction. After a few minutes, he saw *it*.

Near the base of one of the large trees, there was an animal with its right paw caught in a coil of rope fastened to the ground. When the animal tried to pull its paw free, Daniel cried out. The ache in his hand became a sharp pain. Somehow, Daniel knew the hurt the animal felt was being transmitted to him. He just didn't understand how it could be done.

The animal faced him. It snarled and bared two huge canine fangs. It backed up as far as it could, raised its fur like a frightened cat, and faced him. Daniel approached the animal and sat well out of its reach. He began to talk to it. "I won't hurt you," he said. "If you calm down, and let me near you, maybe I can free your paw." Talking to the animal made him feel better. Though he still had no idea where he was, at least he wasn't alone.

He looked into its face as the animal sat staring at him and stopped snarling. It was unlike anything he had ever seen before. It was bigger than a German shepherd and had the same general outline as a dog, but it was covered with a layer of thick green fur. The fur was very uneven, growing several inches high in some areas, and completely missing in other places along its side and hind legs. In those places, Daniel could see its skin, dark brown splattered with even darker brown dots. Its legs were uneven, too. The front legs seemed several inches longer than those behind. Its head rested on a powerful neck that must have been at least ten inches wide and probably a foot long. Its face resembled a bear's, with large eyes and ears. The face of the creature

9

was green except for two patches of brown fur that grew around its eyes, giving it a raccoon's mask. Its green-brown tail moved slowly back and forth while the animal sat unblinking, looking into Daniel's eyes.

Now that the animal was quiet, the pain in Daniel's hand was gone. "Wherever I am, I don't think I'm home," he said to it. "You don't exist in my world. But you're here, aren't you? That means I'm . . . that's impossible, isn't it? People don't fall down on one planet and get up on another. That only happens in make-believe stories. I sure wish you could talk! Maybe you could tell me where I am and how I got here. Listen, I'm going to get up and walk to you. Don't be afraid; I'm not going to hurt you." He rose very slowly and came closer to it. It watched him rise, never taking its eyes off him. When he was near enough to touch it, he stopped, kneeled down, and extended his hand.

A small black nose that seemed lost in the green fur reached out and smelled it the way a dog tests the scent of a stranger. Daniel lowered his hand and grabbed at the cord. It was looped through a stake buried several inches in the ground. He moved the stake back and forth, trying to loosen it without hurting the animal. Finally, the stake popped out, and he freed the paw. He sat before the animal.

"See, I told you I'd help."

The animal poked its head next to Daniel and sniffed his cheek. Then it got up and walked to the base of one of the enormous trees. Looking back once, it began climbing. Daniel watched it go, but soon the animal blended in so well he lost sight of it.

10

He stood there for a moment, staring into the trees, trying to understand what had happened. The pain and buzzing were gone. Obviously, Daniel had felt the pain the animal felt. But why did he hear the buzzing noise inside his head? He wondered if the animal read his mind and knew he wouldn't hurt it. Was that the reason for the buzzing sound? It would explain why the animal remained calm while he worked so hard to free it. He knew that an animal's being able to read his mind made no sense, but nothing since he woke up had made any sense.

He had started to walk away when he heard other sounds. He turned and saw eight men on horseback racing toward him. Though he was relieved to see other human beings and wanted to speak to them, he didn't like the way the horses were bearing down on him. He climbed onto the branch of one of the trees and sat, waiting for the men; there was no reason to run because they could easily catch him. The horses looked like horses, except that their tails were very short. The men wore the same type of clothing he did, and some had swords strapped around their waists, others had them strapped to their backs. They stopped in front of him.

"That was a foolish thing to do," said one of them.

"What was?" asked Daniel.

"Releasing the tomago," he said.

"What's a tomago?" replied Daniel.

"The animal you just let go. It could have killed you."

"Oh, it was just scared. Once it knew I wouldn't hurt it, it quieted down. It wasn't dangerous."

11

"Not dangerous?" said the man as he looked up at Daniel. "Don't you know tomagos are one of the fiercest fighters in Lithia? Their front paws are so powerful they could crush the life out of any of these horses."

"What's Lithia?" asked Daniel.

"What?"

"I said, what's Lithia?"

"What do you mean, 'What's Lithia?' " said the man. "You're in Lithia!"

"Oh, it's a country. I'm lost. I don't know where I am."

"You can say that again," said the man. "If you're not from here, where are you from?"

"Pennsylvania," answered Daniel.

"What's that?" asked the man.

"What's what?" said Daniel.

"Pen . . sil . ."

"Pennsylvania? I told you, that's where I live."

"And where is this Pen-sil-vain-ya?"

"Ahh," said Daniel as he turned and looked around him. He raised one hand to the sky, and then lowered it. "I don't know."

"What do you mean, 'You don't know'?" snapped one of the horsemen.

"I don't know where I am," answered Daniel. "Since I don't know where I am, how am I supposed to know where my home is? That's what 'lost' means. Not knowing where you are or how to get back to where you want to be."

"Then what are you doing here?" asked the man before him.

"I don't know!" said Daniel, throwing both hands in

12

the air and letting out a deep breath. "I'm not being very helpful, am I? I don't mean to be that way. I'm just very mixed up."

"I can tell!" answered the man. "Do you remember your name?"

"Daniel Taylor."

"Well, Daniel Taylor, my name is Artema, and I think you'd better come with us. It's not safe for a boy in . . . in your condition to be wandering about Boen Woods, even if you did escape the jaws of the tomago." He reached up, grabbed Daniel, and lowered him onto his saddle.

"I don't suppose you remember why you're wearing those colors, do you?" asked Artema as they rode.

"No, I don't. Do they mean anything?"

"It means you support Resson."

"Who's he?"

"The regent-king of Lithia. If you were older, those colors would mean you were a soldier, like us. Since you're too young, it means you support him instead of Lauren."

"Lauren?" asked Daniel.

"Have you always been like this?" asked the man.

"No. I was fine until the storm. Then I got hit by lightning and woke up here."

"What storm?" asked Artema. "There hasn't been any rain here for over two weeks."

"Well . . ." started Daniel.

"No, don't tell me," Artema said. "It probably wouldn't make sense. Nothing you've said makes sense. I just hope what you've got isn't catching. Save your answers for Bluecastle."

"Who's Bluecastle?"

"Not who, what. Bluecastle is the capital of Lithia, and home of the king."

As they rode through the woods, Daniel thought about what had happened, and the more he thought, the more he came to the same conclusion. This was not Earth! It couldn't be. There were no tomagos on Earth, no such place as Lithia on Earth, and modern armies did not ride horses and fight with swords. But how did he get here, and more important, how was he going to get home? Just as his stomach began to tell him this might be a good time to get upset again, Daniel got his first glimpse of Bluecastle.

Bluecastle was not what he imagined. It was neither blue, nor was there a castle poking its turrets into the sky. It had a huge wall made of the tremendous trees that grew in Boen Woods. The builders of the city had cut down hundreds of the trees and notched them together like Lincoln Logs. The entire city was ringed with them. The entrance was like a medieval drawbridge, which was lowered when the troops were near.

"Everything's fine," said Artema. "The only one we saw was this boy. There were no rebels." He reported this to a man stationed on a platform raised several feet off the ground immediately inside the drawbridge.

Daniel noticed that the soldiers on the platform held bows and arrows. The arrows, loosely notched in their strings, had curved barbs protruding out of their tips. Those arrows, thought Daniel, would do just as much damage when being pulled out as when they went in.

"Well, take the boy to the king," said the man on the

14

platform. "He should be in the stable playing with his new pet. He ordered all prisoners brought to him before they get thrown into the pit. Though by the time Resson asks to see them again, there hasn't been enough left of them to see." He laughed as he pointed the way.

"What did he mean?" asked Daniel.

"What did he mean about what?" answered Artema.

"About my being a prisoner?"

"It's nothing to worry about. Anyone picked up without being able to account for his presence is always questioned. I don't think you'll meet the inquisitor. If you were a few years older, then I'd worry."

Daniel was about to ask Artema who the rebels were when suddenly he felt a terrific pain in his back. For an instant, he thought Artema had plunged a knife into him; he would have fallen off the horse if Artema hadn't grabbed him. The pain lasted for a second and disappeared as suddenly as it came. Artema jumped down and helped Daniel off.

Daniel rubbed his back, but he didn't feel anything now.

"Be careful," said Artema. "That's the king getting up from the ground. He's been trying to train the mahemuth for over a week. He's going to be in a bad mood."

Daniel didn't have to ask what a mahemuth was. He saw for himself. Next to the man brushing himself off was a horse being held by seven men. And what a horse! She was black; deep, ebony, shining black, and at least the same height, if not several hands taller, than a Clydesdale. But unlike those massive work horses, this one was proportioned like a sleek racehorse. Her black tail, laced throughout with strands of bright red hair, was long and sweeping and almost touched the ground. Her mane was the same, long silky black with touches of sparkling red. That same red flashed in the animal's eyes as the king approached it. This creature was the most beautiful animal Daniel had ever seen. Calling it a horse would be an insult. This breed needed a separate name. Mahemuth fit.

Daniel looked at the man who was walking toward the mahemuth. He, too, was tall, well built, with muscular broad shoulders, and a neatly trimmed beard covering his chin and lower cheeks.

"I'll ride you yet!" said the king.

The mahemuth tried to back away, but seven sweating men held her steady. When Resson hauled himself into the saddle, the men jumped away. The mahemuth reared high on her hind legs and Daniel, watching from outside the corral, screamed. The pain in his back returned, and he fell. When the pain finally stopped, he sat up, wiping a tear from his eye. Artema ran and helped him to his feet.

Resson, too, was getting up. After a moment, Daniel thought he understood what had happened. The mahemuth was hurting, and he was sharing the same pain the animal felt.

"Stop!" yelled Daniel, as the king neared the mahemuth again. "You're hurting her."

"Are you out of your mind," whispered Artema. "No one talks to the king like that!"

But Resson had heard. He turned and walked to Dan-

16

iel. "What I do, and to whom or what I do it, is none of your concern," said Resson. He looked down at Daniel, and then shifted his gaze to Artema. "Who is he, Artema? I don't recognize him."

Artema, who had snapped to attention, answered quickly. "We picked him up on patrol. His name is Daniel Taylor, and he offered no explanation for his presence, sir."

"Hold him, but not in the pit. At least, not until I speak to him again!"

The king turned as Daniel tore away from Artema's grip.

"You don't understand," said Daniel as he ran to block the king's way. "The mahemuth's in pain. There must be something bothering her under the saddle blanket. I felt it. When you put your weight on her, it hurts her."

Resson looked long and hard at Daniel. Then, while the men held the mahemuth, he reached under her stomach, unbuckled the cinch, and threw the saddle and blanket to the ground. Blood dripped from an open wound on the animal's back. He kicked at the blanket and pointed. A soldier raced to it and began searching. When he stood up, he had a bloodied arrowhead in his hand.

"It was in the blanket," said the soldier.

The king didn't look at Daniel for an explanation, but to a man who stood near the gate. Resson pointed to that man, who was grabbed by several soldiers. The man's face paled; he looked like a ghost by the time he was pulled before Resson.

"Did you think this animal would kill me, so your precious Lauren could return unpunished for her crimes? Take him to the pit, and when he has something to say, send for me."

"But my Lord," squeaked the man. "It was an accident. I didn't know. I swear it! I didn't know!"

But Resson had already turned his back and faced Daniel, who was wiping the mahemuth with a cloth. "Artema, bring this boy to my chambers. I'll talk to him now. You," he said pointing to another man, "find Dexter. Have him come to me."

Daniel was led away. Artema walked two paces in front of him, and two soldiers followed behind. They passed a small wooden building with slits for windows. The door was partly open, and several sweaty soldiers were standing nearby, breathing deeply. When Daniel passed the door, he understood why the men were outside. The air from inside smelled like a week-old garbage can no one wanted to empty. Daniel knew from the stench that this was a place he never wanted to visit.

Artema stopped when he reached the entrance to a huge wooden house, several stories high. As Daniel stepped into the house, he heard a scream. He turned around just in time to see the last soldier disappear into the house with the narrow windows and slam the door after him. The scream was cut off. He looked at Artema.

"That's the pit," said Artema. "I hope you never see the inside of it."

Chapter 2

Daniel was in the throne room. Resson sat in front of him, in a chair carved from a single piece of wood. Artema and Dexter stood beside him. Pictures hung on the wall; some of Resson, some of other men and women. There were several spaces where pictures once had hung, but now only vague outlines of the frames could be seen.

The room looked cold. There were no rugs on the highly polished wood floor, and other than the throne, only a few pieces of furniture.

Daniel began his story with waking up in Boen Woods. He decided it was best not to say anything about his real past; no one would believe him anyway. Besides, he didn't trust Resson after hearing him in the corral and saw no reason to have the king accuse him of being a liar. He said he couldn't remember anything before waking up. He felt uneasy. His stomach kept trying to bounce up into his throat, and he was constantly swallowing to get it back where it belonged. Resson could send him to the pit, and Daniel knew it. When he finished, the long, narrow hall was silent.

The man called Dexter finally spoke. "The land of Nivia is far from our borders. I have heard of a province in that country where some people called Empaths are born. These Empaths have a power found nowhere else on Enstor. They can communicate with animals. Not in words, but in feelings. They sense what animals feel. They can send their thoughts into the minds of animals, calming or exciting them. Look at this boy. His hair is almost blond. Most of our people have much darker hair. And his eyes?" Dexter cupped his hand under Daniel's chin and lifted up his face. "They're almost green. He wasn't born in Lithia, I'd bet my life on it. If he is from Nivia, it would explain how he was able to approach the tomago, and how he knew the arrow was hurting the mahemuth."

"But how did he get here?" said Resson, never taking his eyes off Daniel. "And why can't he remember anything except his name?"

Dexter didn't answer immediately. Daniel hoped he'd have an explanation Resson would accept. He didn't want to see the inside of the pit.

"You told me the boy almost fainted when you mounted the mahemuth," said Dexter. "He felt the pain. That's beyond question. It is said that if an Empath is in contact with an animal when the animal suffers greatly or dies, the shock may cause the Empath to lose all memory. If that happened, it would explain his condition."

"Even if what you say is true, it doesn't explain how he got to Lithia. Will he ever remember?" asked the king.

"I don't know," answered Dexter.

Now Resson turned to face Dexter. "I could use a boy like him," he whispered. "For now, he could control the mahemuth. But when he grows, and has a man's skill with a man's knowledge, he could be a valuable asset to me."

Resson put a warm smile on his face as he stepped down. It was the first time Daniel had seen the king smile. The king placed one hand on his shoulder as he spoke. "So, Daniel Taylor," he said, "it seems your past is closed, and we may never find the reason for your journey here. But don't worry. You will find a new home with us. Dexter said you possess a great gift, a gift we will teach you to use wisely. For now, I will make you keeper of the royal stable. It will be your responsibility to care for the animals in your charge. As you grow, we will find other uses for you. You should be happy here.

"Dexter, arrange quarters for Daniel within the manor. I don't want him living outside our compound until I have tamed the mahemuth. Give him the room next to Jeanine's. She'll need some company when she returns. Artema, you are temporarily relieved of your present duties. I am putting you in charge of Daniel. Get him a horse and make sure he hasn't forgotten how to ride. Get him a sword and show him how to use it if he doesn't already know. Do the same with bow and arrow. He must learn to fight with his own skill and not depend on the animals he will one day command."

"Yes, sir!" snapped Artema.

"Leave us now, Daniel. We have business to discuss, and you have a new home to get used to." The king stopped Daniel with a call before Artema could push him out of the door. "I am sorry, Daniel, for the harsh words I spoke when we met. I want you to remember this: I am good to those who follow me. I have no patience for those who don't. We will talk later."

Daniel didn't know what to say. He nodded, as Artema pulled him into the hall. He was confused and still had no idea how he got to this world or how he was going to get home. He knew enough to realize that if some freak accident threw him here, it probably would not happen again and send him back. Unless he found someone to help him, he would be trapped here for the rest of his life. And the only someone he could think of was a magician, a real magician, like a wizard. For a brief moment, he thought of Evelyn and wished she were here with him. He needed to talk to someone as bright as she. No, on second thought, he was glad she wasn't. If she were, Resson would have already thrown her into the pit.

As he followed Artema, he knew he would have to make some decisions about his future. The first thing he had to do was find out if magicians existed on Enstor, and if they did, where he could find them. But until he knew more about Lithia, more about the war that was going on, he wasn't going to ask anyone about people who could do magic. What if there were no wizards, he thought. What would he do then? This entire thing was becoming more than his thirteen-year-old mind could handle.

That night, his first in Bluecastle, Daniel tossed restlessly in his sleep. Waking in the small hours of the night, he jumped off his bed and poked his head out the window. Though he knew he was no longer on earth, part of his mind hoped it wasn't true, hoped that when he woke up in the morning he would find himself in his own bed, in his own room. Now he knew that would never happen. High in the sky above him Daniel saw two moons.

For the next several days, Daniel saw very little of Resson and spent most of his time with Hira, the name he gave to the mahemuth. Artema was always with him, enjoying his vacation from the regular duties of a soldier. Daniel wanted to find out all he could about Lithia, and Artema, who loved to talk, was a good storyteller.

Daniel learned that for the past three hundred years, Lithia had been ruled by queens. Even Artema didn't know why power was passed from mother to daughter, instead of father to son. Eight months ago, Roanda, queen of Lithia, and her husband, King Batten, were murdered. Their daughter, Lauren, was to be the next queen. But rumors saying the assassins were hired by Lauren fanned over the countryside. Though she was only eighteen, some people said she wanted to rule and was tired of waiting for her mother to die. Nothing could be proven until one of the murderers was finally captured. The man was questioned, and before he died, he named Lauren as his employer.

Resson tried to capture Lauren, but she escaped.

Since that time, the country had been in a civil war. Resson, who declared Lauren a murderer and himself regent-king in the name of his ten-year-old daughter Jeanine, led one side. Princess Lauren, who denied having anything to do with her parents' deaths, led the other.

"But who's telling the truth?" asked Daniel. "I've smelled the air near the pit. Resson isn't the nicest person I've ever met."

"How would you feel if your sister were killed and your niece was responsible? Resson does what he thinks is best for all the people in Lithia. People are suffering," he said, looking in the direction of the pit, "but people always suffer in a war."

"I guess so," answered Daniel. "But who do you think killed the queen?"

"I don't," answered Artema.

"You don't what?" said Daniel.

"I don't think."

"What do you mean, you 'don't think'? Everyone thinks!"

"Of course I think, youngster," said Artema. "I just don't think about who really killed the king and queen. I'm a soldier. Even before you came, I had an easy job. I eat well, and my duties aren't that hard. To be perfectly honest, it makes no difference to me who sits on the throne. My life hasn't changed since the war began. Most of the real fighting takes place in Brata, one of the outlying provinces and far away from here. Lauren was raised there, and that's where most of her army is. But don't go telling anyone what I've said. It's our secret."

"But if you know where Lauren is, wouldn't Resson know too?"

"Not that, boy! That's not the secret. How I feel. *That*'s the secret!"

"How you feel about what?" asked Daniel.

"About who rules Lithia!"

Both of them shook their heads and laughed.

Daniel thought about what Artema had told him. If what Resson said was true, then maybe staying in Bluecastle for the rest of his life wouldn't be so bad. But if Resson was lying, Daniel didn't want to use his own strange power over animals to help him. He might even want to help Lauren, but in order to do that, he'd have to leave Bluecastle, and that wouldn't be easy. He had no idea where Brata was, no way of getting there, and no way of getting out of Bluecastle. More and more, it seemed to Daniel that the only way out of his predicament would be for *someone* to cast a magic spell and send him back to Pennsylvania. But the few times he had asked Artema if there were any wizards in Lithia, Artema had just laughed.

So Daniel spent the next week thinking about questions he couldn't answer and taking care of Hira. Artema had told him that mahemuths were very rare animals. Few were ever caught, because of their great speed. Hira was captured only because she was injured when the king's men found her, and she was too weak to fight or run away.

Daniel discovered he could project his feelings into Hira's mind. He had a calming effect on her, and soon she followed him around the corral and gingerly took food from his hand. He talked to Hira. It made him feel less lonely. He missed his parents, his friends, and even his bratty sister. He told Hira everything about himself and his real past. Whenever he spoke, Hira would stand still as a statue, looking at him with her bright red eyes. Sometimes, Daniel had the strangest feeling Hira understood every word he said.

When Hira's back was completely healed, Resson told Daniel to saddle her. He did it, but inside he felt terrible. Hira was like an eagle, born to be free and to follow no one. When Resson mounted, she didn't buck. She stood gazing with saddened eyes at Daniel, who could almost feel the weight of the king on his own back.

Soon, Resson was riding Hira through the streets of Bluecastle, with Daniel in attendance. Though Daniel didn't like seeing the king on Hira, he did like being away from the royal compound, the area set aside solely for the use of the king. It gave him a chance to see Bluecastle. Since he arrived, the only places he had been allowed to go were the stable, the arena where he had lessons using swords and bows, and the living quarters of the king's residence.

Near the outer wall, all the houses were made of wood and were packed as close together as kittens nursing from their mother. Many of the houses had small chimneys. Daniel wondered how the ones that didn't were heated or where those people cooked their meals. But Resson never stopped as he rode, and Daniel had no choice but to follow. The streets were narrow, but wide enough for three horses to ride next to each other, and along both sides of them shallow trenches were dug. Daniel saw people throwing dirty water and garbage into those trenches.

The high wall surrounding Bluecastle was longer than Daniel had imagined when he first saw it. It must have covered several square miles, because many times he couldn't even see it. Deep inside the city, away from the outer wall, the people lived differently. The houses were much larger and farther apart, some with as many as four chimney stacks. This must be where the rich people lived.

When Resson rode through the crowded sections of his city, the people applauded and bowed low when he passed. They pointed at Hira and said finding and training such an animal was a sign from the Creator, a sign proving Lauren had had her parents killed. Resson lowered his head slightly when he heard the praises, but no one ever mentioned the boy who was always seen riding behind the great mahemuth.

A few weeks after Daniel arrived, he finally got out of Bluecastle. Resson was taking Hira on a run through Boen Woods, and Daniel was needed to make sure the mahemuth wouldn't bolt and run away.

It felt great being outside the walls. It took his mind off some of his problems, such as how to escape or how to find Lauren. At midday, they stopped in a small meadow, bare of all trees. The sun shone brightly, and the grass was thick and green. Though Resson remained on Hira while he ate, most of his guards dismounted. Several soldiers walked to a small creek that ran on the edge of the meadow, while others took out the food they had brought and began eating.

Daniel got off his horse and stretched his legs. "It's been a long ride," he said to Artema.

You help me. Me help you, said a voice.

"What did you say, Artema?" asked Daniel. But when he turned, he saw Artema was walking toward the stream.

You help me, said the voice again.

Daniel looked around and saw no one was near him. "Where are you?" he whispered.

You look! said the voice.

At the far end of the pasture, Hira was staring straight at him, pawing the ground with her hoof.

"Did you . . . did you talk?" Daniel said, almost to himself.

You help me, me take you far away, came the answer.

"Wait a minute," whispered Daniel. "Either I'm crazy or you're talking."

Me think, you hear, said the voice. *No need talk.*

It is you, isn't it, Hira? thought Daniel, concentrating on the mahemuth. *I'm reading your thoughts and you're reading mine!*

Yes.

If we could talk to each other like this, why didn't you do it before?

No reason. No help in city. Trapped behind walls, said Hira.

What do you want me to do? thought Daniel.

Me run. You follow. Me take you where you want go. Then, me run free.

Yes, Daniel thought back. *If we work together, we*

28

can both free ourselves. Daniel looked around. Most of the soldiers were relaxing and were too far away from their horses to prevent him from mounting his and racing away.

Now! thought Daniel.

Instantly, the huge mahemuth reared up. Still in the saddle, Resson was caught completely off guard and slid off. Hira brought her front legs down, kicking up with her hind legs just as Resson was about to reach the ground. Instead of falling harmlessly, the king found himself flying through the air, propelled by the powerful kick of the mahemuth.

Hira raced into the woods. Daniel jumped on his horse and charged after her. "See to the king!" he yelled. "I'll catch Hira and meet you back at Bluecastle!" He didn't wait for an answer. He leaned low over his horse's neck and sped after the disappearing mahemuth.

In a few minutes, he was deep inside Boen Woods. He lost sight of Hira. Compared to her, the horse he rode was no faster than a tortoise.

Here, he heard.

Off to the left, he saw Hira waiting for him. When he reached her, he removed the bit from her mouth and replaced it with a makeshift halter.

"Can you take me out of these woods?" he asked.

Where? came the reply.

"Brata," Daniel said.

Where? Hira asked again.

"Brata. It's somewhere in this country. I'm hoping Princess Lauren is there, and I want to find her."

How we find Brata?

29

"I don't know. I thought maybe you'd know."

Brata is man name.

"Okay," answered Daniel as he mounted, "so we're both lost. We can ask directions later. Let's get out of these woods."

Where?

"That way," said Daniel, pointing to the north. "That's in the opposite direction of Bluecastle." Hira began running. Daniel could feel her massive muscles stretch and the surge of power as her hind legs pushed off. He towered over the ground as the wind whistled past his ears. He felt fantastic. Somehow, he had melted into Hira's mind and reveled in the newfound freedom the mahemuth was feeling. This feeling of elation continued as the last trees of Boen Woods faded and they rode onto a long, grassy plain.

For the next four days, Hira carried him across that boring landscape. Hira never tired. At night, Daniel made a bed of grass and slept soundly while Hira ate and slept near him. He managed to find enough berries and fruits to keep him from going hungry, but his stomach was constantly telling him it was time for a decent meal.

On the morning of the fifth day, he wasn't awakened by Hira's gentle nudge. Instead, he was kicked on the sole of his boot and heard a rough voice.

"Get up, kid! You can't expect to sleep the whole day, not with King Resson searching the entire country for you," yelled the voice. "It's not polite to keep our king waiting."

Laughter burst out all around him. He wasn't given

time to sit up as rough hands hauled him to his feet. In the distance, he saw Hira racing away, with several men chasing her.

"You'll never catch her," he said sleepily, as his hands were pulled behind his back and tied.

"We know! But when the king asks if we tried, we'll be able to say yes." Daniel saw he was surrounded by half a dozen men. Their clothes were torn and dirty. All were unshaven and had beards of varying lengths. When he breathed in, he smelled them. It had been a long time since any of them had seen a bar of soap.

"What do you want with me?" asked Daniel.

"Nothing. But the king wants you. He wants you bad enough to offer a reward for anyone bringing in the boy who stole his mahemuth. Since we don't have the mahemuth, we'll see if he'll pay just for you."

"And if he doesn't?" whispered Daniel.

"Well, then we'll either sell you as a slave in Trytandoree or bury you under the ground, so good King Resson will always wonder what became of the boy who stole his property."

Again, the men laughed loudly while Daniel was pushed forward and thrown into the back of an open wagon.

Chapter 3

The rest of the day was horrendous. Daniel stayed in the wagon completely ignored by his captors. He bounced like a loose ball in a can as the wagon rolled over the increasingly rough terrain. Having his hands tied behind him was the worst part. His head slammed against the side or floor several times, and there was nothing he could do to protect himself. When they finally stopped, untied him, fed him, and threw him into a tent, Daniel backed into the corner and fell asleep.

In the morning, there wasn't a single part of his body that didn't scream as he went to a bucket of water inside the tent. Everything hurt! After drinking, he took off his shirt and wiped his neck and chest. It was hot in there, and he wished he could throw away the smelly thing instead of having to put it back on.

He peeked outside and saw two men sitting near a dying fire. When he stepped out, they turned to face him.

"We don't want any trouble from you, boy, understand? Mestir and the others rode to Bluecastle. Until they get back, you stay inside. You don't bother us, we don't bother you."

"I have to go," said Daniel.

One of the men rose and pulled his sword. "If you think you can get past us without being chopped up into little pieces, go right ahead."

"I didn't mean go away," he said. "I meant to the bathroom."

The man laughed and put the sword back. "Behind the tent. And be quick about it."

Breakfast was a bowl of cereal that looked like mud, a piece of bread, and some kind of fruit. It was the size of a lemon but orange-gray in color. He was allowed to eat outside, but neither man spoke to him.

Though the mud cereal looked awful, he ate it. After the first bite, he decided it wasn't bad. It reminded him of something he once had for dessert, Indian pudding. Before he ate the fruit, he was shooed back into the tent. He was about to bite into it, when a voice invaded his mind.

Hungry, he heard.

Daniel looked. He didn't see anything or anyone. Shrugging his shoulders, he opened his mouth to bite when the same voice spoke again.

Me want!

Daniel dropped the fruit and watched it roll on the ground. He backed up until he felt the canvas brushing against his head. Something was inside the tent and wanted the last of his meal. Until he knew what it was, he had no intention of arguing.

33

Then he saw it. A snake! Daniel hated snakes, and having to look at three of them each morning before opening his underwear drawer made him hate snakes even more. His stomach behaved like a Ferris wheel, his legs turned to jelly. Since the snake was between him and the tent flap, there was no way out. He crouched down and backed up, getting as far away from it as possible.

It was hard to see the snake as it moved closer to the fruit. Its color matched the yellow-green grass of the ground. The only thing Daniel was happy about was its size. It was small, eight or nine inches, and thin enough to make its home in a soda bottle, had anyone in this world invented soda.

Daniel watched as it stopped next to the fruit. It opened its mouth and began forcing the fruit in. Its lower jaw dislodged and it slithered forward, pushing the fruit farther into its mouth. Unfortunately, while eating, the snake came closer to Daniel, whose rear fell down as he pulled his legs up and wrapped his arms around them.

Why afraid? he heard.

"Did you say something?" he whispered.

The snake stopped crawling. It actually lifted its head a few inches and looked around.

No one here. Must be me.

"What do you want?" asked Daniel, feeling the Ferris wheel slow down. Being able to talk to the snake made it less frightening.

Nothing. Me feel strange feeling when look for food. Me not feel before. Me come look. Must be you. Me never speak before. Why afraid?

34

"I'm afraid of snakes," answered Daniel.

What snake? asked the snake.

"You. You're a snake."

Me just call me Me. Why afraid? Me no hurt if you no hurt first.

"I've always been afraid of snakes. They crawl on the ground and have fangs to bite with."

Me no fangs. Me no bite. Me spit when afraid. Me afraid of people. People no look where go. Crawl better, can see where going. People step with big feet. Stepping feet hurt. Most time, people no see Me. Me only come because of strange feeling.

Daniel thought about what the snake said. From its point of view, people were just as dangerous to it as he thought snakes were dangerous to him. It certainly wasn't a snake's fault it had no legs. Mice had legs, and Daniel was afraid of them, too. He took a deep breath, trying to convince himself he had no real reason to be afraid of the snake who called itself Me.

"Okay, Me, I'll make sure I never step on you. Do you want to be friends?"

What 'friends'? Me asked.

"Friends are people who help each other and care for each other."

Me no people.

"That's all right. We can still be friends."

You no hurt. You get food. You watch over Me?

"If you promise not to bite?"

Me tell you. No teeth. Me no can bite. Me spit. You no hurt, Me no spit. Me promise.

"What happens when you spit?"

What Me spit, dies. Poison kills.

"What do you eat?" said Daniel softly.

What Me eat before, or things like it.

"Do you ever eat little animals?"

Me never kill food. Only from tree Me eat.

"Okay," said Daniel, "then we can be friends if you want to." Daniel sat perfectly still as Me crawled to him. He wasn't sure if he was doing the right thing, but he needed all the friends he could find if he hoped to get away from the men who kidnaped him. He lowered his hand and let Me crawl into his palm. His hand shook as Me curled up in a small coil, poked its head underneath the bottom coil, and brought its head through the space its body made. Me rested its little head on its tiny body as it watched Daniel. Its tongue, which wasn't forked, flicked in and out, but not very often. Me wasn't slimy, and its scales were very smooth and dry to the touch. Slowly, the Ferris wheel stopped. The jelly disappeared.

Replacing Me on the floor, Daniel told it his story, from the snowstorm to the kidnaping. Me listened without saying anything and Daniel wondered if it understood what he was saying.

After the story, Me looked up. *Me think me know,* it said. *You not from this world. You from other world. Maybe people from other world when come here can talk like you to Me. Maybe people from our world when go to your world do the same.* Me may have been a small snake, and its grammar may have been terrible, but it certainly wasn't stupid.

"That's possible!" said Daniel. "Hira said she didn't

36

speak to me in Bluecastle because while we were in the city, there was no way to help her."

What Hira?

"A very large animal who helped me escape."

Me no know Hira. How she help Me?

"Hira didn't help you, Me. She helped me, Me."

Oh, answered Me.

Daniel shook his head. All of a sudden, something Me said connected with Daniel's mind. "Me, you said you thought if someone from this world went to my world, they might be able to talk to the animals there. Have you ever heard of anyone going to another world? Have you ever heard of anyone who can send people to another world?"

How Me know what people do? Me stay away people. People have big feet.

"I just thought . . . anyway," Daniel continued, "we've got to get away from here before the rest of the men return."

Me go. Me spit.

"No. Don't do that. I don't want to hurt anyone unless it's absolutely necessary. Maybe we could just scare them."

All right, answered Me. *But if they step, Me spit!*

Daniel picked Me up, gently covering it with his palm. Pulling back the flap, he stepped out. The two men were just adding some small branches to the fire.

"We told you, stay in the tent. Now get back and close the flap behind you."

"There's something I forgot to tell you. You might

37

find it helpful if you listen. It won't take long."

"All right," said one of the men, breaking a branch, "sit over here. Just be quick about it!"

"Well, what is it?" asked the other one.

"I'm not from Lithia," said Daniel, putting Me in the grass.

They laughed. "You're right, boy. That's very useful. If we ever need a guide to show us around your home, we'll look you up. Now . . ."

"You don't understand," said Daniel.

"I guess we don't," answered the first man, as he put the branch on the fire. "I mean, we can live without knowing where you're from, can't we?"

"Since you put it that way, no. You can't."

"Can't what?" asked the man.

"Can't live."

"Listen boy, if you've something to say, say it. I'm not in the mood for riddles."

Daniel looked down. Me was still lying there where he put it. "I'm from Nivia, and I can talk to animals." One of the men laughed. "You still don't understand. I know it may be hard, but just listen. I spoke with something that says it's poisonous, and I thought you might want to see it before I tell it it's okay to spit at you." He pointed at the ground just as Me stuck its head up and moved it back and forth between the two men.

They froze. The color drained from their cheeks. Their breathing became shallow. They must have thought moving their chests up and down would cause the snake to attack.

"You're not laughing. Good. I'll take that to mean it

38

was telling the truth. You wait here while I saddle one of the horses. Don't go away." When Daniel rose, one of the men made a noise. He breathed out, and a sick sigh escaped his lips. His eyes looked from Daniel to the snake, but his neck never moved an inch. "Don't worry. If you don't move, it won't hurt you." Daniel left and found the horses grazing nearby. After saddling one of them, he chased the other away. He took a saddle pack and filled it with bread and dried meat. He decided against taking one of the men's swords because even though Artema had begun to teach him how to use it, he was really terrible with it. However, he did take a knife. By the time he was ready, both men looked very ill.

"Which way is Brata?" he asked.

"East," whispered one of the men. "Just don't forget the wyerin," he squeaked.

"What's a wyerin?" Daniel asked as he walked to his horse. The man made a bleating noise and looked at the snake. "Oh, this," Daniel said, returning to pick Me up. Daniel dropped Me into his shirt pocket, mounted, and raced away, never looking back. He rode east, using the sun as his guide. After a few moments, a familiar voice told him to wait. Turning, he saw Hira. The huge mahemuth gracefully trotted to him, with her head and tail held high.

"You waited for me?" he said.

Me no wait. Me sleep. What you want?

"No, not you, Me. Me me. And I'm not talking to you anyway. I'm talking to Hira."

Daniel felt Me moving inside his pocket. Suddenly,

39

its head poked out. But it wasn't green. It was brown, the same cocoa brown as his shirt. "Are you all right? What's the matter? You're not green anymore."

Never green. Always black, like now, answered Hira.

"Not you, Hira, Me," answered Daniel.

When you green? asked Hira. *Never see green people.*

"This is not going to be easy," said Daniel. "It's too confusing." He reached into his pocket and pulled Me out, who coiled around his fingers, looking like a large, brown worm.

Hira lowered her head to sniff Daniel's hand.

"This, Hira, is Me. Don't be afraid."

It big, said Me. *But if your friend, Me no afraid. Just make sure it no step.*

"Hira, Me is a wyerin. It spits poison but without it I couldn't have escaped. Me gets afraid when it thinks someone will step on it."

No step, answered Hira. *But keep in pocket.*

"Fine," said Daniel looking at Me. His eyes began to grow when he saw the wyerin in his hand was losing its color. The brown was fading, and Me was turning into a light flesh tone matching the color of his hand. "What's happening to you, Me?" he said, raising Me to eye level.

Nothing, answered Me. *Me change color. Me always look like ground Me hide in. When no one see, no one step.*

"Fantastic!" cried Daniel. "A chameleon snake. Just make sure when I put you down, don't stay still. I have to know where you are. I don't want to step on you."

You step, Me . . .

"I know," said Daniel. "I step, Me spit. Go back to sleep now." He held his hand over his pocket and watched it slide back.

"Why did you wait, Hira?" He made a mental note to use proper names whenever possible. It seemed that both Hira and Me could hear him whenever he spoke or thought to them. From now on, using the pronoun "me" would make having a conversation very difficult.

We agree. You free me. Me carry you. Daniel expected Me to poke its head up, but peeking into his pocket, he saw Me coiled up, sleeping. Another mental note: the animals couldn't talk to each other. He was grateful for that.

Men come while me sleep. No chance to warn you. Me follow when they stop chasing. Me wait. Now, we go.

After transferring the full saddle pack, Daniel set off again. He thanked Hira for keeping her word. It was a shame people weren't so honor bound. If they were, the king and queen wouldn't have been murdered.

For three days they rode, always heading east. Twice they had to make wide circles to avoid large groups of soldiers. Toward noon on the fourth day, Daniel halted Hira on a high ridge. He dismounted and crawled to the edge. He had heard the sounds of fighting and didn't want to run into any of Resson's soldiers.

Careful, he heard. *You squeeze.*

"Sorry, Me. Maybe you should get out of my pocket for a while. Don't get lost," he said, putting Me in the grass. When he reached the end of the soil, he found himself looking down into a small valley.

41

He saw the final moments of a small battle. There was a wagon train, made up of four wagons. Three of them were the same open kind he had been tied up in. The fourth was covered, looking just like one the pioneers used to cross the North American plains. Most of the soldiers wore the gray and brown of Resson's army, and they were the winners. He saw many bodies near the wagons. Those men also wore gray pants, but their shirts were green and had a white stripe running along the sleeves.

You want Me spit? said Me as it poked its head under Daniel's arm. Daniel jumped, frightened by the sudden appearance of the wyerin.

"Don't do that, Me! Say something before you sneak up."

Okay. Me no do.

When Daniel turned back, he forced his eyes to stay open. It was obvious Resson's men enjoyed the aftermath of the fight. They were passing a small bottle from one person to another. They laughed as they walked from one fallen soldier to the next, killing anyone who was still alive. The laughing became louder when some of the king's men started taunting one soldier they didn't kill. He was standing at the edge of the covered wagon, wearing a robe with a rope coiled around him. The soldiers forced him to watch while the dying men were killed. Daniel couldn't see his face, but his head was held high. The men standing on the ground laughed as they used the tips of their swords to lift up the edge of his robe and peek at the man's legs. Daniel didn't understand that at all.

When the last wounded man was dead, the soldiers tied the prisoner's legs to the wagon. As it began moving away, Daniel scrambled back like a leaping cat. He leaned against the nearest tree and threw up. He had seen people die many times before, but those people were only actors. This was different. This was real life.

Both Hira and Me waited near him. Finally, he straightened himself, walked back to Hira, and drank from the water flask. "Where are you, Me?" he asked. Instead of an answer, he felt Me as it wound its way up his leg and into his pocket. "Hira, we have to free the man they didn't kill. He must be someone important, or else he'd be dead, too. Maybe he knows where Lauren is. The dead men back there must be Lauren's soldiers."

Before he returned to the saddle, he went back to where he had viewed the massacre. He could see the wagon heading away. But only four or five men rode with the wagon. The rest were headed farther south.

"We have to catch the wagon and scare off a few soldiers. Do you think we can?"

Hira's voice came first. *Wait. When night come, we try.*

Me was next. *We do. Me go. Me spit!* it said as it began to slide down Daniel's chest.

"Where are you going, Me?" asked Daniel.

Me go. Me spit.

"Who are you going to spit at?" said Daniel, grabbing Me in the center of its body.

Me looked around. Its tongue darted in and out a few times, but it didn't answer.

Me wait. You tell Me. Then, Me go. Me spit.

Daniel laughed. "You know, Me, I'm very glad you're with us. I'm glad we decided to be friends." He petted it gently as he put it back in his pocket.

"Hira, stay far enough behind so they won't see us. Our only hope is to sneak up on them in the dark."

I catch, she said. *No worry.*

He still had a foul taste in his mouth, like having eaten chalk. But he had to smile. He noticed a subtle change in Hira's speech pattern. Instead of using the pronoun "me," she said "I." That might make things a little easier. The word "me" had taken on a new meaning. It now stood for a feisty little snake who was afraid of being stepped on, and whose answer to any problem was always, *Me spit!*

Daniel didn't ask Hira if she knew where she was going. He trusted the big mahemuth. He was just a passenger and had no say in their direction. While Hira trotted on, he thought. He was beginning to make up his mind about helping Lauren even before reaching her. He didn't like Resson, and he didn't like the men following him. The soldiers killing those wounded men wore the king's colors. He couldn't be part of any force that enjoyed killing so much.

If, after meeting Lauren, he decided she did what they said, then he would take Me and go to Nivia. Unless he found someone to help him get home, he would have to make a new life for himself in this world. But if he believed her, and if Lauren could use his power to talk to animals to help regain her throne, he would help her.

It was early evening when Hira stopped. *Beyond hill.*

44

Daniel didn't ask how she knew. He dismounted and went to look. Walking as quietly as possible, he approached the wagon and saw the robed prisoner still tied in the back of it. The soldiers were busy making a fire and tethering the horses so they could graze.

He backed off and returned to Hira. "We'll wait until they're asleep," he said.

Me wait. Me hungry! he heard.

"I think we should all eat," he said. "Then maybe we can sleep for a while. Me, can you watch for us? Can you stay awake and warn us if anyone comes?"

Me do, Me said.

"Listen, Me," Daniel said after they had eaten, "when the moons are over us, let us know." Moons. Daniel was still not used to seeing two moons in the night sky. But he couldn't ask anyone about them because those same moons would be in the Nivian sky, and he didn't want anyone to suspect his home was much farther away than Nivia. Of the two moons, one Bern, was about the same size as the moon over Earth. The other one, Pern, was much smaller. The strange thing was that the smaller moon revolved around the larger one. During his many nights in Bluecastle, he had often watched the smaller moon circling the bigger one.

Me do. You sleep. Me wake you when moons over Me.

Daniel slept. He thrashed about, for his dreams weren't pleasant. He saw himself reliving the battle he had watched earlier, only this time, it was from the eyes of a bird flying over the valley. From this height, he saw

45

the place where he had lain. But he wasn't there. Instead, an ugly, fat, little goblin sat, licking its thick lips as it waited for the soldiers to leave so it could feast on the remains of the dead.

Chapter 4

Daniel sat up in the night air. He was drenched in his own sweat and pulled off his shirt to let the cool breeze fan him.

Not time yet. Moons not over us, said Me.

"I had a bad dream. Let's see if we can't get this over with now. The sooner we are away from here, the easier I'll sleep."

He put his sticky shirt back on and dropped Me into his pocket. Hira was saddled and ready to go. "You be on guard, Me," he said. "All we want to do is scare them. Understand? Don't spit."

Me poked his head out of the pocket. *Only when you say, Me spit,* it said.

"Good," whispered Daniel as he crept thieflike toward the camp. The fire was very low. Three men lay sleeping around it, while a fourth slept sitting against a tree.

That's the one we'll get, thought Daniel. *If we can*

keep him quiet, maybe I can cut the ropes and free the prisoner before the others wake. Once we're on Hira, they'll never catch us.

Dropping Me a few feet from the sleeping guard, Daniel circled and came up behind him. In the dim light he could just see Me sticking up on the man's boot.

Me, can you make a noise? he thought.

The wyerin answered with a tiny hissing sound. Daniel nudged the guard very gently in the back while asking Me to do it again. The man stirred. When his boot moved, Me hissed louder.

The guard's eyes opened. He wiped them with the back of his hands as he looked around. He didn't see Me. He leaned forward, putting one hand on the ground in order to get up. His face came close to his foot when Me hissed a third time. The man saw it. He froze.

Daniel stepped out and whispered in the man's ear. "You know what that is, don't you? If you move, or make one sound, you're dead. Understand?"

The man never blinked an eye.

"Good. I need some rope to tie you up, and you're going to get it. If you wake up your friends, the wyerin will kill you. I saw how you butchered those men, and you're lucky I don't believe in killing for no reason. If I did . . ." Daniel reached down and picked Me up. He placed it on the man's shoulders. "Remember, if you make one sound, my friend spits."

Me spit? he heard.

No! his mind yelled back. *Only if he makes a noise.*

48

The man rose and walked to the wagon. His head never turned. His legs hardly made a sound as he moved. He returned with the rope and followed Daniel away from the camp.

While he tied and gagged the man, Daniel wondered just how poisonous Me really was. But now was not the time to ask. He dropped Me into his pocket before he returned to the camp and the sleeping prisoner in the wagon. The man was awake. He must have awakened when the guard took the rope. Daniel brought his hands to his lips, and the man nodded. Carefully bending down, Daniel cut the ropes that bound the prisoner's legs to the wagon. Together, they catwalked into the surrounding darkness.

"Can you ride?" whispered Daniel. He kept walking, knowing Hira would find them. He wanted to get far away.

"Why should I go with you?" whispered a soft voice from the darkness within the pulled-down hood.

"You don't have to," answered Daniel. "You're free. I just thought you'd repay me for freeing you by taking me to Lauren."

Why Me want Lauren?

I'm not talking to you, Me, he thought. He lifted his hand up and stilled the wyerin moving in his pocket.

"Why are you doing this? What do you want with Princess Lauren?"

"I want to talk to her. Something I want to ask, that's all."

"How do I know this isn't one of Resson's tricks? You may be young, but you wear the traitor's colors.

49

Resson wants to know where the army is, too. This could be a trap."

"I'm not that young!" said Daniel a bit louder than he wanted. They both stopped and listened. When nothing stirred behind them, he crouched down. "This isn't the place to have a discussion," he said. "Can't we talk later?"

"All right. You can travel with me for a while. Where are your horses?"

Hira? he thought. *Come get us.*

While they stood waiting, the man lowered the hood. Hair fell out and around his shoulders. Daniel looked up and for the first time saw the face of the man he had freed. The man was not a man.

"You're a woman!" he said.

"You didn't know? Whom did you think you were freeing?"

"I don't know. One of Lauren's generals. I told you, I want to find Lauren, and I thought this would be the easiest way."

"You found her," she said. "I am Princess Lauren Sherry Roanda, queen-apparent of Lithia. And who are you?"

"Daniel Taylor." Footsteps behind them made Daniel turn and whirl about, holding the knife in his hand. *Hira,* he thought. *Don't scare me like that!*

Me not scared. Me sleep.

Will you stop that, Me! I wasn't talking to you, Daniel thought.

Stop what? Me answered.

Not now. Go back to sleep, thought Daniel.

Lauren was standing, staring at Hira. "A mahemuth! I've only seen one once in my life. How did you . . ." Lauren looked around and did not see any other animals. "If I take you with me, that means I will . . . I never dreamed of riding a mahemuth!" She touched Hira softly on her nose, just to make sure the animal was really there. Then she turned to Daniel. "Who are you? You got that soldier to bring you a rope without being near him, and I've never heard of a boy taming a mahemuth."

"I told you," said Daniel, "I'm Daniel Taylor. Can we go now? Please?"

Lauren looked at him. In the hazy moonlight, he could just make out her eyes. "General Maston would think I'm crazy, but I am going to trust you, Daniel Taylor. I'll take you with me." She mounted first, and Daniel got up behind her. The saddle was not big enough for both of them, so he sat close behind her, but on Hira's back. "You're a strange boy, Daniel," she said. "Have you any other secrets I should know about? Perhaps a wyerin in your pants pocket?"

Daniel squirmed and would have fallen off Hira if Lauren hadn't reached behind to steady him. "Why did you say that?" he asked.

"I was only teasing," she answered. "I didn't mean to startle you."

"Why tease me with a wyerin?" he asked. As Hira began to trot, he wrapped his arms around her waist and leaned his head on her back.

"There's something strange about you. I don't have

51

to look further than the mahemuth to know that. A wyerin is a strange animal, too."

"Why is it strange? It's just an animal," said Daniel.

"You know wyerins are small, shy animals that only eat fruits and berries, but never any meat."

"Sure, but what's strange about that?" he asked. He had to speak loudly into her ear because Hira had begun running faster, and he was beginning to bounce up and down. He squeezed his arms tighter around Lauren's waist to help keep himself from falling.

"Nothing," she answered. "Nothing, except wyerins are one of the deadliest creatures in all of Lithia. The acidlike venom they spit destroys anything it touches. They aim for the head, and whatever they hit dies within minutes. Don't you think it's strange that the Creator made an animal so timid it kills nothing for food, yet so powerful it can destroy the largest of animals? I think it's just as strange to find a boy outsmarting Resson's soldiers and riding a mahemuth."

By now, Hira was racing, and sitting on her back became easier for Daniel. He rested his head on Lauren's shoulders and closed his eyes, listening to the pounding of the mahemuth's hooves. He must have been really tired because he fell asleep in that position. When someone called out to them, his head jerked up and he saw that it was early morning.

"Halt! Name yourself and give the password." Lauren answered, starting a chain of voices echoing the message that the princess had returned. By the time they broke through the few trees, he saw many men on horses racing toward them. Hira slowed and stopped. Lauren jumped down and walked to greet her men.

Daniel didn't go right away. Instead, he removed the halter from Hira's head. Next, he unbuckled the cinch and took off the saddle. Finally, he took a clean rag from his pack and began rubbing Hira's back. By this time, the princess stood next to him.

"What a magnificent mahemuth," said one of the soldiers standing next to Lauren.

"Riding her was an experience I'll never forget," she said. "She never tired, never slowed, never even lowered her head."

"It's rumored Resson possesses a mahemuth. They say he found it injured and managed to train it," said the soldier.

"He had one," said Daniel from the other side of Hira.

"Who had what?" asked the soldier.

"Resson had a mahemuth," repeated Daniel, bending under Hira's stomach. "This was her." Daniel finished and walked around to join them. "Hira didn't like to have him riding her. She did it only because she had to. Now, she belongs to no one, and no one will ever ride her again unless she says it's okay. Isn't that right, Hira?" he said, petting her nose.

The princess stopped Daniel and spun him around so he faced her. "You stole the mahemuth from Resson?"

In the early morning light, Daniel saw her clearly. Her face was smudged with dirt, but even that couldn't hide how pretty she was. Her hair was a rich, deep brown, though it was very dirty and very tangled. Her eyes were large and the yellow in them matched the color of a spring daisy. He looked at her smiling at him. He began to blush. Daniel was shy around girls, especially pretty ones. "I really didn't do anything. Hira kicked Resson off and I rode her until we got here. Can I ask you something?" he said.

"Sure, whatever you want."

"Did you have your parents killed?"

The men near her gasped. They stood, restlessly moving their feet back and forth.

"Is that what you wanted to talk to me about?" she said. He nodded, still captured by her dirty face and large eyes. "No, Daniel. I didn't have them killed. I loved them too much to see them dead. Some people think I wanted to rule Lithia and didn't want to wait for my mother to die. That's not true. I would have preferred it if my mother had died of old age. I didn't want to be a queen when she died; I didn't know enough and I wasn't ready to wear the crown. But my uncle was ready. Jeanine is only ten years old, and with my parents dead and me accused of their murder, Resson rules in her name until she is eighteen."

"Then Resson is the real murderer," said Daniel.

This time, the princess nodded. "He's the only one who benefits from this war. Do you believe me?"

"I think so," he answered.

"Captain Tigert," she said to the soldier who had spoken to Daniel earlier, "this is Daniel Taylor. He risked his life for me. He's to be treated as if he were my own brother. Make sure everyone knows."

54

"Yes, Majesty," answered Tigert.

Now, it was Hira's turn. She lowered her head and pushed her nose into Daniel's back. He turned and wrapped his arms around her face, rubbing his cheek against her soft flesh.

"Thank you," he whispered to her. "You kept your word. Stay well, stay free. You weren't born to call anyone master."

The huge horse reared high over Daniel's head. She brayed loudly as she pawed the air with her hooves. Lauren, along with the rest of the men, backed up, but Daniel remained rooted to the ground.

Farewell, said Hira. She turned and galloped away.

"You're letting her go?" Tigert asked.

"She was never mine to keep," said Daniel. "She's free now, just the way she was born to be."

"Come on, Daniel," said Lauren. "We're both tired, dirty, and hungry. After we have slept, we'll talk some more. I promise."

He was led to a tent set up near the princess's own. Inside was a cot, a table with bread, cheese, and fruit, and a large tub filled with warm water. Daniel took his clothes off and squeezed into the tub. It was just large enough for him. Me ate while Daniel scrubbed more than a week's dirt off himself. He ate when he finished his bath. Before he crawled into bed, he spoke to Me. "Listen, Me, you can't leave this tent. If someone comes in, you keep still. I don't want anyone to know you're here."

Me know. Me stay. Many people. Many feet. If Me go, people step. If people step, Me spit.

Daniel laughed as he put Me in the corner of the tent. He fell asleep so quickly he never heard Me call, or felt Me as it slithered up the cot's leg and crawled under the covers next to him.

Chapter 5

When Daniel woke up, he saw new clothes, gray pants and a green and white shirt, draped over the chair near the cot. He called Me before getting up and dropped his little pet into the shirt pocket. By the time he poked his head outside, it was late afternoon. The sun, a dull orange-red, was hanging low in the sky. Though it was a beautiful sunset, he turned away. It reminded him of Hira's fiery eyes. "We've slept the whole day," he said to Me. "Let's do some exploring before it gets dark."

Me no sleep whole time. Me wake. Me eat. Me peek.

"You didn't go out, did you?"

Me say before. Many people. Many feet. Me stay.

Daniel laughed. It was hard to think of his innocent poisonous friend as intelligent. It was hard to think of anyone who spoke so poorly as intelligent, but Daniel knew Me was no dummy.

Walking through the large camp was like taking a giant step backward into his own world's history. The camp was a living museum, showing life during the Middle Ages. He saw people turning milk into butter using wooden churns. Weavers had set up portable looms and were turning raw wool into cloth. Soldiers were sharpening their swords on stone wheels. He saw blacksmiths pounding red-hot metal. While he lived in Bluecastle, he had never been allowed to roam free and had spent most of his time near the stable or manor. Even when riding with Resson, he had rarely seen how the common people lived. Now, his eyes ate up the sights, and he loved meandering through the camp.

The people were all dressed in simple clothing. The soldiers wore the same uniform as he did; men wore pants that barely covered their knees, and women wore long plain dresses reaching to their ankles. The colors were all muted—dull browns, grays, reds, or white. Only the green of the soldiers' shirts was bright.

Many animals wandered freely around the camp. He wanted to speak to them only to find out if he could. Besides Me, the only other animal he had ever spoken to was Hira. But he decided against trying. He didn't want to create a scene by having many animals crowd around him. There was one animal with fluffy wool growing on its back. It resembled a sheep, but the fleece was pale brown, not white. Another that looked like a camel was the size of a goat, with a curved back instead of a pronounced hump. A young girl, about his age, was milking it. She smiled when she saw him looking at her. He thought about going over and talking to her. But he decided not to. He smiled back, though, and kept walking. He saw nothing resembling a cat or dog.

Thinking of cats reminded him of Champion, his cat. He hoped his mother wouldn't forget to feed him. He also hoped Evelyn wouldn't tease him by putting her boa near him.

One animal was so strange Daniel had no idea what it was. It looked like a duck, but it had four legs and was covered with pale brown fur. It sported a tiny tail, had no wings, and was no bigger than a skunk. He kneeled down to pet it. It walked close to him, raised its short bill, and sniffed the air. Something in Daniel's scent must have frightened it because it opened its bill, honked, and scurried away.

Daniel stood and breathed the air around him. The smells coming from the various campfires attacked his nose. They were so thick he could almost taste them. His stomach reminded him it was time for supper.

On the way back, he stopped to watch a man cooking some meat over a small fire. While the meat turned slowly on a spit, the man brushed a heavy syrupy liquid on it. The sauce ran down the meat and dripped into the sizzling fire. The smoke blew into Daniel's face.

"Are you hungry, boy?" asked the man.

"Yes, sir," said Daniel.

"Well then, come and eat. We're all family until the cursed Resson lies rotting in the ground, and Lauren is rightfully crowned queen." The man cut some slices of the meat and put them on wooden plates. Next to that, he placed a slice of dark, thickly cut bread. Daniel saw the man pick the meat up with his fingers, so he did the same. As soon as he bit into it, Daniel knew what God fed the angels. After a second bite, he changed his mind.

God didn't give it to the angels, He kept it for Himself. The outside of the meat was sweet and crispy, and the inside was so soft it almost melted in his mouth. It didn't take Daniel long to wipe the plate clean.

The man laughed as he took the plate from him. "You honor me by your appetite. Would you like some more?"

Daniel nodded and watched his plate being refilled. After the third helping he leaned back against a large rock. "I've never had a meal like that. I'm sorry for making such a pig of myself, but I was hungry, and that was good."

The man laughed again. It was a warm laugh that made Daniel feel good hearing it. "What's your name?" he asked.

"Daniel Taylor, sir."

"That's the second time you've called me 'sir.' You honor me with the title. I am Tourcan, a tailor by trade, a soldier by need. And what of you? You are very young to wear the green and white. Have you lost your family?"

"No," answered Daniel. "I came here this morning with Lauren."

"On the mahemuth?"

Daniel nodded.

Tourcan dropped the plate he was holding. "You're the one everyone is talking about? You're the one who saved the princess from Resson's monsters?"

Again, Daniel's head bobbed up and down.

"You could have dined with any in this camp. Any, including the princess herself. And you chose my fire, and my poor meal to share. Who will believe the tale I'll tell?"

Now it was Daniel's turn to laugh. "It was definitely not poor," he said as he patted his stomach.

"Tell me, Daniel," said Tourcan, "what can I do to repay you? If not for eating with me, then for what you did for Lauren."

Daniel was about to say there was nothing he wanted, when he did think of something. "There is something you can do. May I go into your tent? Wait a minute and then come in." Tourcan looked puzzled but agreed. Once inside, Daniel took Me out and made it hide in the corner. When Tourcan entered, the wyerin was hiding in the dried grass tent floor.

Daniel took off his shirt. "I need a slit in the middle of this pocket. Sort of a long buttonhole, only there's no button. It should be about an inch long. Can you do it?"

"Of course I can," he answered. "But why?"

"I'd rather not say."

Tourcan didn't ask again. He went to work doing what Daniel asked. In a few minutes, it was done. He waited outside while Daniel dressed.

"Thank you," said Daniel, standing before Tourcan while Me peeked through its very own peephole. "May I come again?"

"You'll always be welcome in my house, or tent," he said. "I'll look for you."

"Especially around mealtimes," added Daniel. "Oh, one more thing before I go. Lauren doesn't happen to have any wizards with her, does she?"

"Why would the princess want lizards?"

"Not lizards, *wizards*. You know, magicians, sorcerers, wizards. People like that."

"No, Daniel," said Tourcan, laughing. "The princess has no magicians with her. If she did, she would be sleeping in Bluecastle."

"Just thought I'd ask," said Daniel, waving goodbye. He let out a deep breath as he walked away. What if there was no magic on this world? What if he really *really* had no way of getting home? He reached up and petted Me inside his pocket. He decided to look at the rear of the camp before returning to his tent. There was just enough light to get a quick view before the sun sank.

It happened just as he was planning to go back to his tent. A loud, clear, sharp voice exploded in Daniel's head.

Help me, Mommy. Help me!

Me no say that! said Me.

Daniel was confused. Someone was in trouble and calling for help. But why did he hear it in his mind? And how come Me heard it, too? He looked behind the camp, where a large mountain rose to the sky. The plea came again.

Help me. I'm trapped and it's hard to breathe!

Up, that way, said Me.

Without stopping to get someone to help him, Daniel started running on a small path that snaked up the side of the mountain. The higher he went, the more urgent the cry sounded. Whoever was in trouble needed help immediately.

62

The sun was down now, and the moons were no more than pale light bulbs in the eastern horizon. It was then Daniel learned something else about Me, who now sat on his shoulder. It could see very well in the dim haze the moons cast over the path. It knew exactly where to go and guided Daniel quickly along the path. But soon Daniel had to stop. He bent down, taking deep breaths.

When they began again, Me told him to leave the path and begin climbing up the side of a small rise. *Careful,* Me said.

Daniel climbed, kicking loose rocks back to the path.

There, said Me, using its head to point.

Daniel moved to his left and found himself standing over a small crevice filled with stones. Me said the weakening call for help came from under those rocks. Daniel began throwing the stones away, trying to uncover the body Me said was underneath. There was a small opening, no bigger than a few feet across. There had to be a child under the rubble because the opening was too small for an adult. Daniel wondered why a child would be so high in the mountain, and why there were no adults looking for it. As the rocks went flying, he heard the voice.

Hurry! I'm hurt.

"I'm going as fast as I can," he yelled. Now he came to a single, long, flat stone, about a foot in length and twice as wide. It was wedged into the sides of the crevice. The child must be trapped beneath it. That stone, which was very hard to move, had saved the child's life by keeping the mass of rocks from crushing it. Daniel worked hard. Finally, he managed to get one hand under the rock, and raise it high enough to brace himself against the hill while putting his feet on the stone. By pushing his feet against the stone, he was able to move it. He looked down into the small prison the rock had created. The two moons were higher now, giving him enough light to see. There, in the bottom of the pit, was a cat. It was big; about the size of a large puppy. It looked like a Siamese, black face and ears, with shades of gray and white along its body. There was a rock pinning its paw.

Daniel reached down, his feet stretched out to keep the rock from falling. When his hand neared the cat, it hissed and beat the air with its free paw.

"Now listen," said Daniel. "I've come a long way to get you out of there, so stop that nonsense. I'm not going to hurt you!"

The cat looked at him. It tilted its head and gazed at him with one closed eye. Then it sat, sphinxlike, waiting for him to remove the rock.

Again he reached down. This time, the cat was silent. Daniel removed the stone from its paw and lifted the cat out. It was difficult holding the cat and at the same time trying to get out of the crevice, but he did it. As soon as he put the cat down, it began to lick its paw. He petted it on its head, but the cat paid no attention.

"You're a very pretty cat," he said. "Next time, be more careful."

No cat. Kitten. Cub. Young one, said Me. *You, Me, leave. Parents come.*

"What!" said Daniel. "You're a kitten? That would

mean when you grow up you'd be the size of a mountain lion. Imagine, a Siamese lion. Well, little one, I've got to go." He stood up, wondering for the first time why this animal could speak in complete sentences. But he didn't have time to wonder long. He heard a fierce hissing growl. In the moonlight, he saw the cat's parents, two huge animals racing gracefully toward him. Instinctively, he turned to run. His foot slipped and he fell. Before the lion-cats could reach him, his head hit the ground, knocking him unconscious.

Chapter 6

The sun was up when Daniel opened his eyes. His body ached. The stone bed he lay on wasn't very comfortable. Me sat on his stomach, raising itself on its own body.

You come, Me spit, Daniel heard. *You go. You no hurt.*

He looked and saw he was surrounded by four of the Siamese mountain lions. Each faced him from a different direction. They must have known about Me because they were far away.

Is it true you mind-speak? said a voice. He noticed one of the cats beginning to sit up. It was beautiful in the sunlight, with shades of gray, black, and white all blending on its slender body.

Yes, he answered. *I heard someone calling last night. I came to help.*

We know. The little one was my cub, and because you saved his life, you still live.

You forget Me! Me said. *You no come close. You come, Me spit.*

Yes, that too, answered the cat. *But even with your guardian, we could have killed you.*

Daniel stood up, holding Me in his hand. "Thanks," he said to it as the wyerin coiled around his palm.

It is very strange, said the cat. *We have always mindspoken, but never with other creatures. Your friend has told us a curious tale, and we must talk with the clan before making any decision. Also, my mate told me not to harm you. You saved the life of our youngest.*

How come you speak so well? asked Daniel. *The other animals I've spoken to don't.*

I told you, answered the cat. *We have always mindspoken. This is not new to us. But come, you must follow us to our clan site.*

I can't go with you! answered Daniel. *I've got to get back to the camp. I've got to see Princess Lauren.*

If you do not come, we will attack. Your friend may kill one of us, or even two. But you will die from those who are left.

But why? Why must I come with you?

You have seen that we live. Will you come or not?

Daniel saw two large fangs hanging in the cat's mouth as it stretched and yawned. It wasn't fooling when it said it could kill. So he started off, following the large cats.

Soon, he was walking next to the one who spoke with him. Me slept in his pocket. The cats promised they wouldn't hurt either of them as long as Daniel followed. Since Me believed them, Daniel did also.

All day they climbed, twisting and turning deeper and deeper into the mountain, and farther and farther away from Lauren. While he walked, he spoke with the cat next to him.

"I sense you're upset. Why? I haven't done anything to you."

Have you forgotten what your kind has done to us? said the cat.

"I don't know," answered Daniel. "I come from far away."

You are a strange human, for not only do you mind-speak, but you do not know the prison your kind has forced upon us. It's not you I dislike, answered the cat, *but your people. Once, we were many. Our clans lived in every part of the land. But you humans hunted us and there was never a reason for those killings. We never attack unless provoked. Your kind did not seek food; they killed for pleasure. They enjoyed the chase and seeing my clan dead at the end of an arrow. Our numbers became so few we fled to places like this, places humans never come. Our lives are not easy here. The prey we hunt for food is scarce in these mountains. We would like to leave and return to the forests that were once our homes. But we cannot. Your people must think we are all dead, and as long as they do, we are safe from their arrows. It is better to be hungry than dead. You are the first of your race to see a samkit in many years.*

"Is that your name?" asked Daniel. "Samkit?"

That is what we call ourselves. I am Bantu.

Toward evening, Bantu told him they were almost

68

there. Daniel was tired. His legs hurt, and he wanted to rest. Except for a brief stop, he had been walking all day.

There, said Bantu. *We have one last rock to climb. Our home is on the high ground overlooking this path.*

"I can't climb that. It's too steep."

I will help you. Grab my tail. I will pull you up.

"I can't do that!" answered Daniel. "That will hurt you."

The samkit turned to face him. *And how would you know what it feels like to have your tail pulled? Do as I tell you! Cubs, they always think they know best!*

Daniel didn't argue, and with Bantu's help, he scrambled over the boulder. Once on the top, he saw the samkits' home. The ground was flat, with trees and rocks jutting out everywhere. There were many samkits lying in the dying sun. When they saw Daniel, they got up and sat facing him. One of them came toward him.

Is it true you mind-speak?

Yes, answered Daniel.

Then I want to thank you for saving my cub.

That's okay, said Daniel. He reached out to pet the animal when Bantu hissed. He didn't want Daniel to touch his mate.

The she-cat walked to Bantu, and the two samkits rubbed their cheeks together. Daniel heard a low, rumbling sound like a running motor. They were purring!

Another samkit approached. It hissed and bared its fangs. *Why have you brought this killer of samkits here? Have you forgotten how to use your teeth?*

Daniel stepped back, away from the advancing samkits and closer to Bantu. Me poked its head out of its window, but didn't say anything.

I do not need to be reminded by you, Goether, what my teeth are for, answered Bantu. *Come any closer and I will show you what I remember.* He, too, hissed. *But if you think you can kill this one before the elders decide, then do it. Just do not look to any of us for help.*

Help! What help would I need? said Goether. He uttered a low growl and stepped toward Daniel. Me came halfway out of the pocket and flicked its tongue at Goether.

You come, Me spit. Me spit, you die, it said.

Daniel reached down and petted Me behind its head. Me was certainly no coward. Goether knew what Me was, for he jumped back as though he had just stepped on hot coals.

How is it you, too, speak to us? Bantu's mate asked Me.

Me no know. Me never do before. Only when Danyell come, Me talk. Daniel smiled when he heard Me pronounce his name. He continued stroking Me as he followed Bantu. Goether didn't come near them. Me crawled up Daniel's chest and draped itself over his neck, facing the hostile samkit walking behind them.

Daniel was led to a small clearing and told to sit in the center. All around him, the handsome samkits sat, forming a complete circle.

Worthmor, you are the oldest of the elders. Hear what I say. I speak for the human who is not yet out of the cub stage himself. He saved the life of my small-

70

est. Is his death the way we repay him? Daniel recognized the voice of Bantu's mate.

One of the animals got up and walked toward her. It was an old cat whose black patches of fur were speckled with white hairs. Daniel noticed a Z-shaped scar on the samkit's shoulder. It reminded him of something, but he didn't know what. *Tamara, cubling of my mate's youngest, it is not what I wish,* answered Worthmor, *but what is best for the clan. If he were to go free, his people would know we have not vanished from the land. The hunts would begin again. Not only would our clan suffer, but the other clans hidden in places as remote as this would also be in danger.*

But Worthmor, it is not . . . began Tamara.

No! came the reply. *Even before the man-cub arrived the council decided.*

Me, who was rubbing its head under Daniel's chin, spoke. *You come. Many die.*

How are you called? asked Worthmor.

Me, said Daniel.

Not you, said the samkit. *Your protector.*

That's its name, answered Daniel. *He is Me. Or she. I never asked it its sex.*

Well, Me, listen carefully. You guard that one, and we accept that. Loyalty is a commendable thing. But will you allow that loyalty to end your life? Some of us will die. That, too, we accept. But the man-cub cannot survive. If you go now, you will not be harmed. If you choose to stay, you will die.

Me crawled up Daniel's neck and went on top of his head. *Me no go. Me stay.*

71

"Wait a minute," said Daniel. "Don't I get a chance to speak? It's my life! The least you can do is listen."

We will listen, said Worthmor.

"What if I can arrange it so you won't have to remain hidden in places like this, and no one will ever hunt you again?"

How can you do that? asked Worthmor.

He told them about Princess Lauren who would be queen of Lithia once she defeated Resson. "When she's the queen," he said, "I'll ask her to make a law forbidding anyone from ever hunting or killing your people again. I saved her life, and if I ask her to make the law, she will. I know she will."

And if Lauren does not win? asked another voice.

"Your secret will still be safe," he answered. "I could never tell anyone about you, knowing what would happen. If Resson wins, I'm going to leave Lithia. When I go, your secret goes with me. But I'm betting she will win. Won't you take a chance? You have so much to gain, and so little to lose. I promise. I would never tell, knowing it would mean your deaths."

How do we know he speaks the truth? How can we trust this human cub? asked Goether.

A mind-meet, said Tamara, walking to Daniel, who reached up and pulled Me out of his hair. *I call for a mind-meet,* she said again, sitting in front of Daniel. *We will see if he speaks the truth.*

So be it, answered Worthmor. He, and the other sam-kits, moved closer, making an even tighter circle around Daniel.

Do not be afraid, said Tamara. *If you spoke truly,*

you have nothing to fear. Daniel nodded because he felt a pain in his head. It moved inside him, following the same serpentine course Me traveled when the wyerin was in his hair. He wanted to raise his hands to his ears, but he couldn't. He remained still, staring into Tamara's eyes. He knew the samkits were causing the pain. Then the pain grew and burst like an exploding firecracker.

Just before he fainted, he heard Worthmor whisper words that made no sense to him. *A human cub from another world? The mind-send? How can a cub . . . Bantu, he must be protected. This one must be protected.* Then Daniel heard nothing.

When Daniel opened his eyes, he was lying on the ground. The moons were up and he watched Pern as it slowly circled its big brother Bern. The moonlight from both moons was bright enough to light up the mountain. When he turned his head, he saw two samkits, Bantu and Tamara, resting nearby. The only sounds he heard were chirping crickets, and Me was peacefully sleeping draped around his neck. Before he could speak, a dark shadow covered him. He looked up and saw that the smaller moon was now directly between him and the larger moon, blocking the light. He stretched and watched the edge of the large moon grow bigger as the small one continued its endless journey around it. He wondered how many times a night this tiny eclipse occurred.

"What happened?" he asked, as he sat up.

We had a mind-meet, said Bantu. *We forced open your memories and looked into your past. We saw you spoke*

73

the truth and would not betray us. We may not share the same faith in this princess-queen as you do, but we will gamble she will do as you ask. There is only one thing you must do. You must promise never to tell that our clans mind-speak and can communicate with each other.

"I promise," said Daniel.

Good. Tamara and I will come with you. Much has happened since you left your people. We will have a long journey if we want to find your Lauren.

"What do you mean?" asked Daniel.

Tomorrow will be time enough. Come, we will show you where to sleep the rest of the night, said Bantu.

Before lying down in the small cave they showed him, he ate some berries growing along the edge of the clan site. There weren't very many of them, and though Me was full when it went to sleep, Daniel was still hungry.

The pace was slow as the samkits guided him back to Lauren's camp the next day. But the camp was no longer there. The morning after Daniel began his climb, there had been a battle. The samkit who was sent to watch the camp reported that many humans attacked the ones who sheltered beneath the mountain. The ones who were there first defeated the others, but when the battle was over everyone left. Now, the only thing Daniel saw were the mounds of dirt showing where the dead were buried.

"Then we'll have to catch them," said Daniel. "Do you know which direction they took?"

Yes, answered Bantu, *but it will not be easy. We can travel only at night because I do not want anyone to see me.*

No one see Me, said Me. *Me stay in nest.*

No, Me, said Tamara. *Bantu didn't mean you. He meant him, or rather, us. No one but you and Daniel can ever know we live.*

But he say Me, said the wyerin, poking its head out of the tiny door.

I didn't mean you. I meant me, said Bantu.

But . . . started Me when Daniel interrupted.

"Don't worry about it, Me. Why don't you go to sleep?"

Me sleep, it said, and it pulled its head back.

The next seven days weren't easy for Daniel. Most of their nights were spent in walking, following the fading scent of the moving army, while during the day he foraged for fruits and berries. Bantu scouted in front of them, warning if anyone was near. Tamara always stayed by Daniel's side when they traveled, and one of the samkits always rested nearby while the other hunted for their food. The only time he was alone was after one of the samkits made a kill, and the one staying with Daniel went to eat. Then protecting Daniel was left to Me. On the seventh day, they were caught in a terrific rainstorm. Bantu found a tiny cave and they huddled together, waiting for the storm to blow itself out.

The next day, all scent of Lauren's army was gone. They were lost. Since it made no difference which way they traveled, they began following the path offering the greatest amount of protection for the samkits. That way, they could travel during the day, too.

Several days later, Bantu came racing to them. *Men fight ahead,* he said.

Daniel followed him to a stand of bushes. Peeking through the branches, he saw a detachment of soldiers riding over a hill, heading away from him. The soldiers were wearing the green shirts of Lauren's army, but they were too far away for his voice to reach. He looked back to see whom they were fighting. There was a wagon, turned on its side, and near it lay a man. Blood covered his face and shirt.

"Wait here," he told the samkits. He stood up and walked to the wounded soldier.

"Water," said the man in a rough whisper as Daniel helped him lean against the wagon. Looking over the contents of the wagon, he found a leather flask. He held it while the man drank.

"You're a young one," said the man. "They left me for dead and took the rest for prisoners. Did you come to finish the job?"

Daniel could see him look at his dirty green shirt. "I mean you no harm," he said. "I'm from Nivia, and I only borrowed these clothes because mine were torn." He had seen the gash in the man's chest and knew he was dying. There was no reason to say anything to cause him more fear.

"If you don't follow the bloody princess, whom do you swear to?" he whispered.

"I don't swear to anyone. All I want is to go home."

"Then look for her. She was picking flowers or some such fool thing when we were surprised. I guess it saved her life, though."

"Who?" asked Daniel.

"Jeanine," said the soldier, closing his eyes.

"You mean Resson's daughter?" asked Daniel.

"Yes. Find her. We were trying to sneak her through Brata. We didn't think they'd bother a small band like us. We were wrong. Take her to Bluecastle. Keep her out of their hands. If they find her, they'll kill her."

"Why would Lauren's soldiers kill her? She's just a child, isn't she?"

The man drank again. He coughed, and waited until he was breathing easier before continuing. "You really are a foreigner, aren't you? Resson rules in her name. With her dead, he loses all claim to the throne. Lauren, as the only surviving female of the Roanda line, must be given the crown, even though she killed to get it. If Jeanine dies, the murderer wins." He raised his hand and clasped Daniel's wrist. "Find her. Keep her safe. Keep her out of Lauren's hands. Return her to Blue . . ." He never finished.

Daniel had to pry the man's hand away from his arm. He shuddered, feeling an icy chill race down his back. He had never seen a dead man this close before. He found a blanket and covered him.

Before he could warn Bantu and Tamara that Jeanine was somewhere in the area, he heard a scream. It was a high-pitched yell, sounding like a broken siren. It reminded him of one of Evelyn's tantrums. The samkits must have found Jeanine. Then, there was silence. Within seconds, there was another, even more powerful yell. Daniel thought for an instant the samkits were eating her alive. He raced off in the direction of the sound.

Don't hurt her, he thought.

We are not even near her, answered Tamara. *We*

77

*came upon her by accident, but the cub thinks we see
an easy dinner.*

When Daniel caught up with the voice behind the
screams, he saw a little girl, hair down to her shoulders,
wearing a simple dress similar to the ones he saw in
Lauren's camp. The samkits were about twenty feet
from her, trying to ignore her by licking themselves. But
the screams went on and on, a river of sound bellowing
from her tiny throat. When she saw Daniel, she stopped
mid-scream. He walked toward her, past the samkits.
That's when the screams started again.

Daniel put his hands over his ears to muffle the
sound.

You're going to have trouble with that one, said
Bantu.

Tell me something I don't know, he answered.

Tell what? said Me. *Me have nothing to tell. Me
know Me hungry. But that all.*

No, Me, said Daniel. *Not you. Me! Stay inside my
pocket. I don't want her to see you, too.*

Okay, Dan-yell. Me stay.

Good, he answered, cupping his hands even tighter
over his ears.

Chapter 7

Daniel stopped trying to calm the hysterical girl. Every time he opened his mouth or came close enough to touch her, she let out another howl. Bantu couldn't take the noise and went to scout in the direction of the long-gone soldiers.

Daniel decided the best way to get Jeanine to calm down was to do nothing. The girl was having a tantrum, and he wanted no part of it. For once, he was grateful to his sister. She was a screamer, too, especially when she didn't get her way. Jeanine would stop eventually, just as Evelyn always did. So he left, taking Tamara with him.

Jeanine's screams didn't die out suddenly. They continued, but instead of being long and drawn out, they became short and quick. Tamara watched her from a hidden spot while Daniel returned to the wagon. He found some travel bags and stuffed them with as much food and clothing as he could. Then he put Me behind the wagon so it could eat without Jeanine seeing. The last thing he did was cover the body of the dead soldier with rocks.

By now, Jeanine had stopped yelling and stood watching him. She said nothing, but her head constantly moved from side to side. When Daniel finished burying the man, she spoke to him.

"Why did you have to kill him? Why didn't you just take him away like the others?" she asked.

"I didn't kill anyone," answered Daniel. "In case you haven't noticed, the only weapon I have is a knife. Besides, I had no reason to kill him."

"You do kill people!" she yelled. "You follow Laurie. Everyone who does wears shirts like that."

"I don't follow anyone," he said. He decided not to tell Jeanine the entire truth. He didn't believe what the dying man told him and wanted to bring Jeanine to Lauren. If she came willingly, it would make things much easier.

"Then why do you wear her colors?" asked Jeanine.

He sat and pointed for her to do the same. He offered her some food, and she, sitting very calmly now, ate what he gave her. He watched her chew. Her tear-stained cheeks were dirty, and her large brown eyes looked only at the ground between them.

"I don't belong here," he said. "My home is far away, in Nivia. That's where I'm going. I lost my memory and couldn't tell you why I'm in Lithia even if you wanted to know. I couldn't even tell the king, and he did want to know." She didn't even look up when he mentioned the word *king*. "I began in a place called Bluecastle. Have you heard of it?"

She looked at him and nodded.

"When I was there, I learned about the war for the first time. I left, trying to get home. I was kidnaped on the way by some people who wanted to sell me in Tryando, or some place like that."

"Trytandoree," said Jeanine.

"That's it. Anyway, I escaped. I met a girl who brought me here. She was a princess. A real princess! I stayed with her army for a few days. That's where I got this shirt. But I told you, all I want to do is go home. So I left. A short time ago, I found the wagon and heard you screaming. You've got some voice, you know?"

That caused her to smile. "I was all right until those animals attacked me. I hid during the fighting. I never cried out, not even when Mersa fell."

"Those animals are samkits. And they didn't attack you. They found you and were watching you until I got there."

"That's not true!" she said, standing up and throwing the pebble she was holding at him. "They would have attacked me if I hadn't screamed. I scared them into staying away. And they aren't samkits, either. There aren't any samkits anymore. They ate people. That's why they were killed."

"If there aren't any samkits left, then what are they? Bet you can't answer that one!"

"Well . . ."

"By the way, my name's Daniel. What's yours?"

"It's . . ." She stopped in the middle of the sentence. "I'm not telling."

"All right, don't," answered Daniel, standing up. "But I have to call you something if we're going to be traveling together. Do you like the name Evelyn? I remember having a sister named Evelyn. About your age, too. Ten, right?"

"I am not ten!" she yelled, stamping one foot. "I'm almost eleven!"

"How almost?" asked Daniel.

"I'll be eleven in ten months."

"Oh," said Daniel as he looked at her and smiled. Her cheeks began to get red and she turned away. "Okay," he called out, "you're right, you're almost eleven. But you're wrong about the samkits. They don't eat people, and they aren't all dead. If you promise not to scream, I'll ask them to come out."

"How can you ask them anything? Everyone knows you can't speak to animals."

"I can, sort of. I'm an Empath. That means I can communicate with them. Not so much in words, but feelings."

"I know what an Empath is. I'm not dumb!"

"Then do you promise not to scream?"

She nodded and he called Tamara. The samkit came out of the bush and stopped before them. Jeanine stared at her. She reached her hand out hesitantly, like a child quietly stealing a cookie before dinner. When Tamara stretched out to smell her, Jeanine pulled the hand away.

"She is beautiful," she said. "I've never seen anything like it before. I wonder what she is."

"I told you," answered Daniel. "She's a samkit."

"No, she's not. Samkits are all dead."

Daniel shook his head. "She and Bantu are the last ones left. They're coming with m . . . I'm taking them to Nivia. They'll be safe there. I'm trusting you to keep this a secret. If people find out there are two samkits alive, someone will try to kill them."

Jeanine didn't say anything. She just kept staring at Tamara.

"I'll take that as a yes, okay? Come on. We'll stay together until we find someone who can take care of you. I can't leave you here by yourself."

"What if I don't want to go with you? I can take care of myself."

"You don't have to come. You can stay here if you want to. But I'm going. Coming?"

"All right," she answered. After walking in silence for a while, Jeanine said, "How come you're not asking me a lot of questions?"

Daniel smiled to himself. He remembered from when he was much younger all the times Evelyn had come to him whining, "I've got a secret!" It used to drive him crazy trying to guess what it was. Then, when he got older, he just ignored her. That annoyed Evelyn so much she would end up yelling the secret at him. "If you want to say something, you will. If you don't want to say anything, you won't."

They walked in the same direction as the soldiers. Though Jeanine stopped being afraid of Tamara, she always managed to keep Daniel between her and the samkit. They saw Bantu several times, but the male cat didn't return until late that evening.

For the next few days, they walked. The ground rose in a series of rolling hills not high enough to be called mountains, but rocky enough to stop farmers from biting the soil with plows. Aside from the scurrying animals, they didn't see anyone. Walking over the rough ground was hard, and they had to stop to rest often. Jeanine, who still didn't trust him, never told him her real name. But she stopped complaining after the second day.

Daniel did most of the talking. He told her as much as he could without breaking his promise to the samkits. He told her he met the samkits in the mountains, and the two animals decided to come with him. Jeanine still insisted there were no samkits and tended to stay away from them. But once or twice, when she thought Daniel wasn't looking, she petted Tamara.

Tamara took a liking to this girl who had to work up the courage to pet her. Bantu scolded his mate, saying she missed her cubs and wanted someone to mother. Tamara wouldn't listen and stayed close enough to her so Jeanine could pet her if she wanted to.

Daniel told Bantu he thought it was cute. Each one, Tamara and Jeanine, needed something only the other could give. Though Bantu didn't like to admit it, he said Daniel was probably right.

The only problem was Me. It had to remain hidden all the time, peeking out when Tamara and Jeanine walked in front of them. It left Daniel's pocket only at night, to eat and stretch itself.

It was early morning on the fifth day when Daniel was abruptly awakened. Hands gripped him by his shoulders and pulled him to his feet. It took a moment for him to realize what was happening. He heard a voice, and when he didn't answer immediately, a hand slapped him across the face.

84

"Who are you? What are you doing here?" the man asked. Daniel's eyes roamed. There were seven or eight soldiers, all on horseback, all wearing the brown and gray of Resson. There was no sign of either Bantu or Tamara. One of them usually hunted during the pre-dawn hours, and both must be far away eating. Me just began to move in his pocket.

Stay, Me, he thought. *There are too many.* Me stopped moving.

"Well, boy?" repeated the man.

"I'm Daniel Taylor, and this is my sister, Evelyn. We're trying to get home. Our wagon train was attacked several days ago. We've been wandering around ever since."

"And just where does home happen to be?"

"Bluecastle," said Jeanine.

"You expect us to believe that?" said the soldier who had hit Daniel. "Your tracks are leading away from Bluecastle, not toward it."

"Can't you see we're lost!" said Daniel. "I just told you we've been walking around here for days looking for someone to help us. You're the first people we've seen."

Once again the soldier's hand whipped out and struck him. "Don't get smart with me, boy. You wear the green of the witch who would rule. Watch your mouth or I'll cut out your tongue!"

"You leave him alone!" said Jeanine, who came to stand by Daniel.

"Well, if that doesn't beat all," said one of the men on horseback. "The girl's protecting her brother.

Shouldn't it be the other way around?" Everyone but Daniel and Jeanine laughed.

Daniel put his arm around her shoulder and pulled her to him.

Jeanine broke away from him. "You're just big bullies," she shouted, "picking on two kids. When my father finds out what you've done . . ." Jeanine scrambled back to Daniel when the soldier raised his hand as if to hit her.

"Don't say anything," Daniel whispered. "Don't tell them a thing."

"I will if I want to!" she whispered back.

Daniel shook his head as he put his arms around her again. Jeanine stared up at the soldiers. She leaned back and put her hand over Daniel's. Strange, Daniel thought. He was beginning to like this little girl. For all her brattiness, she had spunk! If only she weren't so . . .

"All right, you two," said another soldier, "you'd better come with us. You, boy, ride behind him. Hand the girl to me."

"Don't be afraid," whispered Daniel. "Tamara and Bantu will find us. They'll help us escape."

"I'm not afraid," she whispered back. But from the way it sounded, Daniel doubted if even Jeanine believed it.

Daniel thought to his two friends while they rode. *Bantu! Tamara! Can you hear me?*

Me no speak to cats, said Me.

No, Me. I was asking if they heard me, Dan-yell. Hearing Me calmed him. Just knowing he had an innocent bomb in his pocket made him feel better.

86

We hear both of you, answered Bantu. *We returned too late from our hunt to warn you. We are following and will be near if you need us.*

That made him feel even better. He had an army of his own. Though it was small, it was very deadly. Soon he saw where the riders were taking him. There was a camp roped off between two hills. It consisted of six or seven tents and a corral holding several more horses. They dismounted and were brought before the camp commander. He was a fat soldier with a well-rounded stomach that kept him from seeing his own feet. He was unshaven, but the stubble couldn't be called a beard. The shirt he wore was dirty and covered with grease spots on the chest.

"Well, now, what have we here?" he said as he munched on a piece of bread.

For a second time, Daniel told the story he made up. The fat man laughed. He started to choke and had to wait for someone to bring him a flask. After he drank from it, he spoke again. Daniel could smell what the man drank on his breath.

"You don't expect me to swallow that?" he said. "Next, I suppose you'll be telling me you want a feather-bed so the tooth fairy can find you. You're just lucky I have other things to keep me busy this morning. We'll talk later, and if you haven't changed your story and told me the truth, maybe your sister will. Do you know, watching someone you love slowly cut up into little pieces does wonderful things for the memory. Think about it while you wait. Throw them into the holding tent."

"You can't do that!" shouted Jeanine. "You stand for the king! Resson wouldn't like what you're doing. When he finds out you threatened me, he'll fix you."

The commander got to his feet. He lifted Jeanine up by her collar and slapped her hard. She rolled away, and Daniel ran after her.

"You little worm," the fat man said. "Do you think Resson cares what I do? I'm considered nice compared to him. Were he here, he'd be slicing your brother into pieces by now. I'm going to wait until after lunch."

"That's not true!" shouted Jeanine. She broke away from Daniel and went back to the commander. "Resson's a good man. He's only king because Lauren killed the queen. But he's ruling for his daughter."

The man laughed. "You really are simple. Maybe you do live in Bluecastle. Listen, girl, Resson rules for himself. The best news he could get would be his daughter's dead."

"That's not true," said Jeanine softly.

"Girl, with Lauren and Jeanine dead, Resson must marry again, have a female child, and wait for the child to become a woman. He could rule until he's an old man. With his daughter alive, he only rules for a few more years." He laughed again, a short, vicious sound that made Jeanine back up to Daniel. "Listen to me," he said to his men, "I've been talking politics with a baby instead of getting on with my work. Throw them in the tent with the others. Then bring me one of the men we caught yesterday. Maybe he knows where Lauren is. The rest of you, get out of here and continue patrolling this area."

Daniel and Jeanine were led away and pushed into a tent that stood in the center of the compound. The soldiers who brought them grabbed one of the men already inside. They closed the flap on the way out, leaving only a slit in the top to let light in. It was hot and smelled of stale sweat. Two other prisoners were sitting inside. They looked up, but said nothing. Daniel took Jeanine's hand and led her to a corner.

"It's not true," she whispered. "What he said about Resson. It's not true, none of it."

"Maybe," answered Daniel. "When I met the king, the first order I heard him give was just what the fat man said. Resson ordered someone tortured until he talked. I don't think the man lived very long. I was with Resson, and I was with Lauren. There's a difference. I asked Lauren if she killed her parents. She said no, and I believed her. Besides, there was no reason to have them killed. All she had to do was wait. She'd be queen eventually. But Resson did have a reason. With the queen dead, and the blame falling on Lauren, he became the king. If you think about it, what the fat man said makes sense." Daniel decided to take a chance and wanted to let her know she could trust him. "With you and Lauren dead, Resson could rule for the rest of his life. Did you ever think of that?"

In the dim light, he saw her eyes open wide. He waited for her to speak but she said nothing. Suddenly, like a glass being struck by a flying rock, the silence of the tent was shattered and a scream filled the air.

"Let him die quickly," said one of the prisoners.

"Please," they heard someone cry from outside the tent. "I don't know where Lauren is. I don't know!" Obviously, the fat commander didn't believe him. The soldier screamed again, once. After that, everything was quiet. Jeanine hid her face in Daniel's shoulders and cried.

The flap was suddenly thrown back, forcing the sunlight into the dark tent. Daniel had to shield his eyes to see who stood there. It was the commander. "I really didn't believe him until the end. But it was too late. Maybe one of you know," he said to the two remaining soldiers. "Think about it while I have something to eat. All that work made me hungry."

When he left, Jeanine wiped her eyes and whispered. "You knew who I was all the time, didn't you?"

"Yes," answered Daniel. "The man I buried told me before he died. I hoped to convince you Lauren didn't kill her parents. I want to take you to her. If you spoke with her, maybe you'd believe. I think the fat man has done the convincing for me."

"Mersa said Lauren would kill me if she caught me. I believed him. Now I don't know what to believe. But what can we do now? If I tell them who I am, they won't listen. Even if they did, they might kill us anyway."

"Don't tell them," answered Daniel. "Just keep pretending you're my sister until we find Lauren. You forgot we have two friends nearby and they'll help us escape. We'll get out of here." He kissed her on the top of her head and hugged her tightly. It was strange, but while Jeanine was returning his hug, he thought of his real sister back home. Brat or not, he missed her.

He broke away and crawled to the two men. "Are you hurt?" he asked.

"Not yet, son. But don't ask us later. I doubt that we'll be able to answer."

"I won't have to ask. We're getting out of here," he said. *Bantu,* he thought, *can you hear?* He purposely left out the pronoun.

Yes, came the reply.

Can you see the camp?

Yes.

How many men are there?

Seven.

Will you help us? There are two men inside the tent with Jeanine and m . . . myself. They will help, too.

For a long time, there was a silence in Daniel's head. He knew the samkits were deciding. So far only he and Jeanine knew about the samkits. He hoped that Bantu would let these two men know, too. *We will help,* he heard. *Tell the men to take off their shirts. We will know not to hurt them.*

Daniel looked at the two soldiers. "I have some friends outside. There are seven soldiers left in camp. My friends are going to attack. Will you help?"

"How many friends?" asked one of the men.

"Enough. But take your shirts off. That way, they won't hurt you."

"Why?" asked the other man as he pulled off his shirt.

"I can't explain now." Turning his back, Daniel moved to an empty corner and took Me out. *Me, I need help. Slip out of the tent and find the big, fat man. When I tell you, spit at him.*

Me go. Me spit, it said as it disappeared under the tent.

Me, be careful, thought Daniel. *Don't get stepped on.*

Me be careful.

"And don't miss!" whispered Daniel to himself.

How Me miss? Too fat to miss.

"Get ready," he told the men, as he walked to Jeanine. "No matter what happens, I want you to stay here."

"But I want to help, too."

"There's nothing you can do."

"I'm going to help!"

"The only thing you're going to do is get a spanking if you come out before I tell you. And don't think your screaming is going to stop me. Bantu and Tamara don't need help." He put both hands on her shoulders. "I don't want you hurt, okay? Please, stay here!"

Me ready, he heard.

We, too, answered Bantu.

"Are you ready?" he asked the two men. They moved to the flap, and knelt down, waiting for Daniel to give the word.

"When you hear a scream, charge," Daniel said. *Now, Me. Spit!* he thought.

A second passed, and then he heard it. A loud, bellowing yell. *Now!* thought Daniel to Bantu. *Attack.*

92

"Let's go!" he yelled to the other two men as he charged out of the tent. Looking up, he saw one of Resson's soldiers running straight for him with a tight smile on his lips and a naked sword in his hand.

Chapter 8

Daniel dove, rolling when he hit the ground. The swinging sword missed, but the soldier raised it again and ran after him. Daniel got to his feet just as Bantu jumped past him. The large cat's claws raked across the soldier's chest and sharp teeth muffled his dying cry. Within seconds it was over, and Bantu raced on, looking for another man to kill.

He saw Tamara running after a man who was trying to escape. She jumped on him, bringing him down with her weight. One bite in the back of his neck, and then she was up. The man didn't move when Tamara left.

The horses were crying wildly, trying to jump over the corral made of cut bushes. *Don't go near the horses,* thought Daniel. *We'll need them to get away from here.* Since there was nothing more he could do, he went back to tell Jeanine what had happened. He was pushed into the tent by one of Lauren's soldiers. The other one raced in behind him.

"You won't believe this," said one of the men. "Even though there aren't any more samkits alive, there are two of them out there killing anything that moves. I don't mind fighting, but I like to know I've got a chance of winning. Those animals, I'm not fighting."

"You don't have to," said Daniel. "They're the friends I told you about."

"They are *what!*"

"They are my friends. I'm an Empath from Nivia. I found them and they're coming home with me. They'll leave this camp when they finish because they don't like people. They saved your lives, you know."

"You don't have to remind us. If it weren't for them, we'd be the ones screaming now."

"Then you'll help them?"

"They don't need our help. But if there's anything we can do, you have our word it'll be done."

"I want you to promise never to tell anyone you saw them. They may be the last two samkits alive, and I don't want anyone hunting them. They'll be safe once we reach Nivia."

The two men looked at each other. "We didn't see anything, son."

"Thanks," said Daniel.

By now, there was an eerie silence coming from outside. Even the horses were still. *All is done,* Daniel heard Bantu say. *We will be near you, but do not look for us while you travel with others.*

They promised they wouldn't say anything, and I believe them, replied Daniel.

You will go with them until you find out where Lau-

ren is, said Bantu. *They will lead you to other men, men who have not promised.*

"You get the horses," said one of the soldiers to Daniel when they left. "We'll check to make sure everyone is dead and collect some swords." It took several minutes for Daniel and Jeanine to saddle four horses and walk them to the center of camp.

"Don't come any closer," shouted one of the soldiers. "Lead the horses back the way you came. We'll meet you by the corral."

Daniel saw the two carefully backing away from the other end of the camp. "What's the matter?" he yelled.

"There's a wyerin somewhere around here. The fat pig must have stepped on it. Go back the way you came. We'll meet you outside the camp." When the soldiers reached them, everyone but Daniel mounted.

"Come on, son. We've got to get away before the other soldiers return. We may not have much time."

"I have to get something," said Daniel. "I'll just be a minute." Before the man could protest, Daniel headed back into the camp. *Me,* he thought. *Where are you?*

On tree.

Which tree? asked Daniel.

Green tree.

Me! This is no time for jokes. How can I find you?

Near man Me spit. You come. I tell.

Go to the dead man. I'll meet you there. When he reached the fallen soldier, he bent down and took the man's knife. Me was sitting on the man's arm. Daniel picked Me up and dropped it in his pocket. "You did well," he said. "I'm proud of you." As he turned, he

96

looked at the man's head. His face was gone. Where cheeks, eyes, and nose should have been, there was nothing but bare bones. Me's poison had dissolved the man's flesh. Daniel's shoulders shook as though the icy wind of the blizzard back in Foster Woods were blowing on him again. He now knew how deadly Me was, and why men stopped breathing when they saw it.

As soon as he was on a horse, the four of them raced away, heading deeper into the rolling hills. They rode quickly, forcing the horses to run dangerously fast over the rocky terrain. No one spoke, but the soldiers constantly glanced over their shoulders. As he listened to the rhythmic pounding of the horses, he thought of Hira. He wondered where the majestic mahemuth was now. A shout made Daniel look up, and he saw half a dozen men, wearing green and white, coming toward them. In a short time, Daniel and Jeanine were in another camp.

The captain of this camp, a tall, lean man named Laster, listened to the two men. They kept their promise, never mentioning the samkits. Instead they made up a believable story about the enemy camp thrown into confusion when someone stepped on a wyerin. The soldiers said they escaped then.

When it was Daniel's turn, he told the story about being from Nivia and wanting to go home. Only now, he said, after seeing what Resson's men could do, he wanted to find Lauren to offer her his services. He asked Laster if he could spare a man to take them to the princess.

"I wish I could," answered Laster, "but I can't. First, I'm too short-handed now. More important, I have no idea where our main army is. Lauren's constantly moving while we try to consolidate our forces. You saw what being captured means. If I don't know where Princess Lauren is, I can't be forced to tell. I'm afraid the only thing I can do is to point you toward central Brata. You might find her there. And even if you don't, you should at least be safe from Resson's advance."

"Is Resson coming here?" asked Jeanine.

"Yes."

"But why?" asked Daniel. "Why would he risk everything by coming here? Bluecastle is safe from attack, isn't it?"

Laster dismissed his men, and the two nameless soldiers who rode with Daniel said goodbye. Laster knelt down and drew a circle with one flat side on the ground. "Being from Nivia, this land must be new to you. This is what Lithia looks like. High mountains run the entire length of this curve. They surround Lithia. All except here," he said, running his finger along the straight edge. "This part is bordered by the sea. Great reefs and jutting rocks lie in hundreds of places along our coast. It makes landing a ship on our shores very risky. That, plus the mountains, has isolated Lithia from the rest of the world."

"But what has this to do with Resson coming here?" asked Daniel.

"I'm coming to that," Laster said. He drew a line near the end of the circle that touched the straight seacoast. "This triangle is Brata. It's a small province, one of the smallest in Lithia. Princess Lauren was raised here, and none of the people believe she murdered her parents. As long as Lauren remains free, this war will drag on. It might take years. The trouble is Resson doesn't have years. You see, Brata has the only safe harbors along the entire seacoast. Goods Lithian merchants bought in other countries are being piled up in warehouses in our harbor towns. Those goods are wanted by the rest of Lithia, and as long as Resson claims the throne, the merchandise isn't being delivered. Soon the rich nobles in the other provinces will begin to miss those things. They will demand that Resson do something about it. If he can't, then maybe they'll ask someone who can."

"You mean Lauren," said Jeanine.

"Yes. Our reports say Resson's massing his entire army for a direct assault on Brata. He will try to crush our army and take control of the harbors at the same time."

"Then we'll make for the seacoast," said Daniel. "If we can't find Lauren, we can at least find a ship to take us to Nivia."

"That might be best, Daniel," said Laster. "You can stay the night. In the morning we'll load you up with supplies. I wish you good traveling."

Later that evening, when Jeanine and Daniel sat alone by their small fire, she asked him a question. "How come you didn't tell them who I was? They probably would have tried to find Lauren."

He moved closer to her and placed another stick in the fire. "Do you remember what the fat man said? He told us Resson would be happy if he heard you died. The fat commander might have killed you."

99

"I know," said Jeanine.

"What if one of these men believes the same thing? That it would be better if you were dead?"

"Why would they want me dead?"

"The man I buried when I found you said that with you dead, Lauren would be the undisputed queen, and even if she had killed her parents, your father could no longer claim the throne."

"If that's true, wouldn't it be better for Lauren if I were dead?" she said.

Daniel pulled her around by the shoulders so they sat facing each other. "I want you to reach Lauren. I want you to talk to her and make up your own mind. I believed her, and I want you to believe her, too. But just to be on the safe side, we don't tell anybody who you are until we find her. I don't want anything to happen to you."

"Why?" she whispered.

"I don't know if I should tell you."

"If you don't . . . I'll scream!"

"This is a mistake, and I know it." He shook his head as he said, "I care about you and I don't want you to get hurt."

Jeanine stared at Daniel for a long time. The shadows on her face danced as the flames of the fire jumped up and down. "All right, Daniel. We'll go to Laurie, and I'll talk to her. And thanks for caring. It's nice to know. But don't think because you like me I have to listen to you. I don't, you know, not if I don't want to."

"I know," he said. Something bothered him as he hugged Jeanine. It was what he had just said about caring for her. He had never said that to the real Evelyn and now it was too late. Since he left Bluecastle, every time he asked about magicians, people just stared or laughed. It was slowly sinking into his head that whatever magic had brought him to Enstor would not be able to send him home.

"But tell me," said Jeanine. "Why are you doing this? You're not even from Lithia."

"I don't think you'll like this, but I think your father is wrong. He's causing a lot of suffering, and from what I've heard, it's all based on the confession of one man. Don't you think you'd say anything if you were being tortured?"

"But if Lauren didn't kill her parents . . ."

"Your father did," finished Daniel. "I once asked Artema about the assassin they caught. Artema never saw the man. If your father is the murderer, then he could have made up the whole story about the killer and his confession."

"Maybe you're right, Daniel, but I'll have to think about it. Good night," she said as she rolled over on her blanket and went to sleep.

The following day they ate a hearty breakfast, said goodbye to Laster and his men, and rode off. When they could no longer see the tents, Jeanine veered from the easterly path Laster had told them to follow. She started to cut across country, making a trail of her own. They were no longer traveling south, but northeast.

"Where are we going?" asked Daniel, riding next to her and following her lead.

"I think I know where Laurie might be. There's a

101

place we used to sneak off to when I came to visit. It's called the Valley of Mirror Lake. It's a huge valley hidden between two of those mountains Laster told you about. To get there, you have to ride through a very narrow opening. Once inside, the valley is really flat, and in the center of it is a large lake. The valley walls are so high the wind hardly ever blows there, and the water is so still we could always see ourselves perfectly in it. Laurie loved that place. We used to sit by the shore and comb our hair, just looking into the water. If I were Laurie, that's where I'd go."

"The samkits!" he shouted. "I forgot about them!" *Tamara, Bantu, are you near us?* He wasn't answered in mind-speech. He heard a growl and saw the two samkits coming over the hill they had just climbed. Jeanine jumped off her horse and ran straight for Tamara. She knew Bantu didn't like to be petted, so she hugged Tamara as though she were her long lost teddy bear.

"Listen, Daniel," she said, planting a kiss on a cold, wet nose as big as her face, "she's purring!"

Daniel laughed as he dismounted. He grabbed the horses to prevent them from running away, and when they calmed down, he walked to Jeanine.

"We're back together," said Jeanine, leaving Tamara and sneaking up on Bantu. Before the samkit could retreat, she grabbed him around the neck and rubbed her face in his furry cheek. "Your whiskers tickle," she said.

Can't you control this cub? he asked Daniel.

You're a big male, said Tamara, joining them. *Is this little one too much for you?*

I do not care for humans, answered Bantu. He could

102

have easily thrown the girl aside just by moving his head. But he stayed where he was and let Jeanine scratch him above his ear.

Jeanine was now trapped between the two overgrown kittens, each wanting to be scratched. Daniel would have liked to pet the samkits, too, but he didn't. Jeanine had had several hard shocks during the past few weeks, and he didn't want to spoil this by getting in the way. For now, at least, the two samkits were hers.

But the moment didn't last. Daniel saw dust rising from the trail they had just left. Warning everyone, he and Jeanine ran to their horses while the samkits disappeared.

Four men follow, said Bantu. *They are riding fast.*

Are they Lauren's or Resson's? Daniel asked.

They are men.

Do they have a stripe on their arms like me?

Me no have stripes now. Me all one color.

No Me, not you. Me! I know where you are.

They have no stripes, answered Bantu.

"Let's go!" he yelled. They jumped on their horses and raced away. When he turned, he saw four horsemen pounding after them. The ground became rocky. He knew he should have slowed down, but after another quick backward glance, he urged his horse even faster.

Jeanine yelled as her horse stumbled and threw her. Daniel reined in and jumped down. He reached her just as one of the horsemen turned and headed directly toward them.

Chapter 9

The soldier swerved just as Daniel pushed Jeanine back to avoid being trampled. The rider pulled up sharply. The four soldiers formed a tight circle and smiled as their horses came closer and closer to the two sitting on the ground. Daniel recognized one—he was one of the same men who had captured him before. He must have been out patrolling when the samkits attacked.

The soldiers started talking, asking Daniel a series of quick questions. But Daniel wasn't listening. Instead, he was thinking. This was the second time in two days that he had been captured and he didn't like it. Eventually, he or Jeanine was going to get hurt. It finally dawned on him that he was stuck in this world, and that there were no sorcerers who could say a magic word or cast a magic spell and send him home. This world would be his home for the rest of his life. If he wanted to stay in Lithia, if he wanted to help defeat Resson, it was time he rallied his army. Two samkits, one wyerin, and one ten-year-old girl did not have to be afraid of four soldiers.

Bantu, Tamara, he thought, *it's time we started fighting back, time we did something to help Lauren. Maybe these men know something she should know. I know you don't want to be seen, but everyone will see you when we find Lauren. Being seen by four men before Lauren sees you may be the price you have to pay to free all the samkits. Will you help us again?*

We will do what we must to protect you, answered Bantu.

Daniel stood up, swinging Jeanine behind him. "I'm sorry," he said. "I wasn't paying attention. Did you say something?"

"What!" yelled the man, who made his horse raise its front feet slightly off the ground. "You have none of Lauren's traitors to help you escape now, boy. I'll enjoy killing you. Or maybe we'll let you watch us kill your sister before you die."

Daniel still held Jeanine behind him in a backward hug. She peeked out and stuck her tongue out at the soldier. "We're not afraid of you," she yelled. "We have friends who'll get you if you hurt us!"

The rest of the men chuckled as they backed away, giving their leader room.

"It's easy for you to threaten us while you're on your horse. Are you afraid to get down?" said Daniel.

The rider's cheeks turned red. He backed off quickly, jumped down, and waited for one of his men to grab his horse. While the other men dismounted, he pulled s long sword. "I'll enjoy this. I won't kill you liately. I want it to be slow."

Daniel didn't know why, but whenever he tried to speak to regular horses, they never answered. Maybe he couldn't talk to them, but maybe he could make them feel what he wanted them to. He thought of the tomago he helped a long time ago. He visualized it standing in front of him, growling and snapping its jaws, and projected that image toward the soldiers' horses. The horses whinnied and pulled against their reins. Their eyes reflected pure terror though nothing was there. They reared high, striking the air with their hooves. The men backed away, and the horses raced off, leaving their owners dumbfounded.

"I made the horses do that," said Daniel to the soldier who had the sword in his hand.

"We'll get them back," said the soldier stepping toward him. "We'll use your horses to get ours."

"I don't think you understand," said Daniel. "I made those horses run away. I was there when your men died in that other camp you took us to, and if you don't drop your sword, when we leave, you'll be in the same condition as your fat captain."

"That was an accident. We don't know about the rest, but Dagoon scared a wyerin."

"No, he didn't," said Daniel reaching into his pocket. "He didn't frighten a wyerin. A wyerin looked for him, and I told the wyerin to do it. This is the wyerin! This is the one who did it." He took his hand out of his pocket. Me was wrapped around his fingers, head high, tongue moving slowly in and out.

Jeanine, who was still behind him, jumped away. She fell, and instead of getting up, slid farther away in a sitting position.

The three men who were far away also jumped back. One of them dropped his sword and raised his hand over his eyes.

The advancing soldier stopped. "So you are the one who tricked one of our men into believing you controlled a wyerin? You were the one who released the witch? We thought he was lying and even our hot knives wouldn't make him change his story. We were sure he was a spy."

"So you killed him."

"If not for being a spy, then for being stupid. No one tames a wyerin. What you hold must be some harmless cousin of that worm." Without warning, he lunged, sword up, moving quickly toward Daniel's wrist.

Daniel may have been caught off guard, but Me wasn't. From the air above Daniel's hand, a small round ball of purple liquid appeared. Its sweetness tickled Daniel's nose. The purple ball of poison flew straight into the man's eyes. The sword dropped. The man fell, grabbing his face as he screamed. The dusty ground grew muddy with his blood. Jeanine screamed, too, putting her hands over her ears to stop the other's yells from reaching her. It took less than a minute for the man to stop rolling. The three others turned and ran.

Stop them, Bantu, Daniel thought.

A loud hiss stopped the men when they reached the top of the hill. Bantu and Tamara sat facing them. The man closest to Bantu stopped short, causing the others to

107

bump into him. They all fell and made no attempt to get up as the two samkits sat like sphinxes in front of them.

"There are no samkits left," said one man to his friends.

"Why does everyone say that whenever they see them?" asked Daniel. "Of course they're alive. If they weren't alive you wouldn't be seeing them, would you? However, if you think the samkits aren't real, then get up and run away. If they're only in your imagination, they can't hurt you." To put a period on Daniel's last sentence, Bantu hissed. No one moved.

"Good," said Daniel. "I should let them kill you, or let this wyerin spit at you after what you've done."

Want Me spit? asked Me.

No, Me, thought Daniel as he let the wyerin wrap itself around his fingers. *You're a good wyerin, and you saved my life. These men won't hurt us.* He petted Me by holding his finger still while Me continued to weave around his hand.

"I'd like to know a few things before you leave," he said.

"Anything. Just ask us. We'll tell you whatever we know," said one of them.

A short time later, Daniel did let them go. They carried no weapons and had to leave their boots behind. They would have a long, slow walk back. Daniel wondered if when they told their story about seeing two samkits, anyone would believe it.

The three men didn't know much. In a week's time, they were going to break their camp and rendezvous with a much larger army. They had heard rumors Res-

108

son would be there, but they hadn't been told. Daniel was satisfied they had told him the truth.

Finally, he turned and walked back to Jeanine, who had found a rock to hide behind. "Don't you come near me with that thing!" she screamed.

"There's no reason to shout. I can hear very well." He stepped toward her but when she screamed, he backed off.

"I can shout if I want to! Stay away from me!"

Daniel sat on the ground and waited. Jeanine's eyes were glued on Me, who still rested on his hand. After a minute, he dropped Me into his pocket.

"How long have you had it?" she asked.

"Since before we met."

"You never told me!"

"I know. I didn't want to scare you."

"I'm not scared of anything," she yelled.

"If you keep this up, Jeanine, you're going to get a spanking. You're beginning to sound just like the spoiled brat you were when we first met."

Jeanine crossed her arms in front of her chest. "All right, tell me."

"Look, you trusted me when . . ."

Me trust you. You friend. Me like.

Daniel didn't talk back to Me, but just started over again. "You believed m . . . You believed it when I told you the samkits wouldn't hurt you, didn't you?" Jeanine nodded. "Then believe it when I say the wyerin won't hurt you either." *Me, this is my friend, Jeanine. I think you should meet her now.*

Me poked his head out of his pocket door. It looked

around before it slid down to the ground and slithered toward her. She raised her legs, pushing herself as far back as she could go. Me stopped before her and stuck its head up. Tamara came to them and lowered her head to sniff Me. Me's tongue must have tickled the samkit's nose because she sneezed, blowing Me backwards. Me fell over itself. It quickly coiled into a tight ball and brought its head up from the inside of the coil to rest on its body.

Jeanine laughed and immediately clamped her hands over her mouth. Daniel knew she did that because she was supposed to be angry.

Why do? asked Me.

I'm sorry, answered Tamara. *I didn't mean to frighten you. It was an accident.*

Daniel picked Me up and replaced it in his pocket. "See, even Tamara isn't afraid. Please, Jeanine. Don't be afraid. It won't hurt you."

"I don't want to touch it," she said.

"You don't have to do anything you don't want to." He lowered his hand and helped her up.

"All right," she said. "Daniel, do you still like me?"

"It was a mistake telling you in the first place. Now, you'll probably hold it over my head for the rest of my life. Yes, Jeanine. I still like you. I guess I like you a lot."

"Who are you, Daniel?" asked Jeanine. "I don't think you've lost your memory. I don't even think you're from Nivia."

"I'll tell you as we go." As they rode, he told her about his life in Pennsylvania, about the snow storm

110

and the strange lightning that hit him, and finally waking up in Boen Woods. He told her everything except that the samkits could talk to each other. He even told her why the samkits were with them, and the law he was going to ask Lauren to make.

Jeanine said she'd do whatever she could to make sure Lauren made the law the samkits wanted, and when the law was made, she'd make sure it wasn't broken. He told the samkits what she had said, and they thanked her.

"What about Me?" Jeanine asked.

"What about you?" he answered, not knowing what she meant.

"No, silly," she said. "Not me me, your friend, Me. Does it want something from Laurie, too?"

Daniel began to laugh. "No. The only thing it wants is to be fed when it's hungry and not to be stepped on. As I told you, if you step, Me spits."

Who spit? Me no spit. No one step in new home.

Daniel kept forgetting that both Me and the samkits could always hear him whenever he thought directly to them or spoke to anyone. But as far as Me was concerned, hearing half of a conversation always led to problems.

No, Me, he said. *No one spit. You go back to sleep.*

Me sleep, it said. Daniel felt the wyerin move around in his pocket as he spurred his horse to a faster gait. He was anxious to find the valley Jeanine was looking for and see the young queen again.

Chapter 10

Daniel's tiny army was lucky. They saw no one for the next week. Bantu ranged before them, and Tamara was always in sight behind. Jeanine picked the general direction, but the actual trail they followed was up to Bantu. The only time they pleaded with the samkit was when they saw a small lake hidden behind some trees. Both Daniel and Jeanine wanted desperately to bathe and wash their clothes. Though Bantu disagreed, they camped early near the deserted shoreline.

Even Tamara was drawn into the water. When she went to drink, Jeanine splashed her with a wave that thoroughly soaked her. She charged after Jeanine, but the young girl stood her ground and splashed some more. Bantu stayed near them, continually walking through the woods to make sure no one approached. He finally joined them as they sat by their fire, warming themselves, drying their clothes, and eating from their dwindling supplies.

Daniel was happy. The last week had been an easy one. He only hoped the next few would be the same. Shortly after they began the following morning, they saw Bantu running to them. That could only mean trouble. Daniel stopped and waited for the large cat.

There are many men before us. They do not wear the stripe, and they go in the same direction as we. This is not good. If they have riders watching from behind as Tamara does for us, we will be seen.

"Can't we go around them?" asked Daniel.

There are too many. Come. Leave the horses and follow. You will see for yourselves.

He and Jeanine trotted after Bantu until they came to some large rocks. Peeking over the top, they saw what Bantu meant. There were more than many. There must have been over two thousand. Clouds of dust were kicked up as the army broke camp and prepared to leave.

"Father!" cried Jeanine, pointing into the camp. "See that flag in the center? That's our family emblem. If it's there, Father must be there, too."

From their hidden seats, they watched as Resson's army packed everything into wagons and began moving away. "This isn't good," said Daniel. "If Resson's here, the rest of his army will be coming to him. He can't make a major assault with those soldiers. As long as we're traveling in the same direction, we run the risk of being caught. We have to go back. Maybe we can wait until nightfall and . . . " He stopped when Jeanine pointed again.

Behind the now-mounted army, behind the wagons

filled with packed tents and supplies, marched long lines of men. They marched five wide and at least fifty long. A rope, looped around the neck of each prisoner, kept them all in single lines. They wore green and white, though many shirts were so caked with blood and dirt it was hard to tell. They walked silently. A line of mounted guards rode on each side of them.

"We can't just go, Daniel," said Jeanine. "We have to do something to help them."

"We're only two people, two samkits, and one wyerin. What can we do?" They waited until they were sure everyone had gone before they returned to Tamara and their horses.

"What if we wait until dark?" said Jeanine. "We might be able to sneak into the camp. Even if we only get a knife to them, it might help. They could cut their ropes and run away. Some of them will escape. And if Father sends his men to look for them, he'll have to stop his army and stay in one place for a day or so."

"And while they're camped, we can go around them. Once we're far out in front, I don't think they'll catch us. We can move much faster than an army. Jeanine, you're a genius!" He pulled her toward him and messed up her tangled hair even more. "You have to be prepared for another possibility. If Lauren's soldiers decide to attack while everyone is asleep, your father could get killed."

Jeanine stared back at him. "I was never sure if Father knew what the men in his army did. But he's there. He has to know what's happening. He has to know how his soldiers are treating those men. I know he's my

114

father, but I've never seen this part of him. He's too cruel to rule Lithia, even for the few years it takes me to grow up. We have to find Laurie. She has to stop him. She has to."

Daniel kept holding her. Her eyes began to blink and turn red. Tears appeared along the sides of them. He didn't say anything. He just hugged her.

He told Bantu what they wanted to do, and when Jeanine was ready they left, stalking the army that had vanished over the horizon. They moved slowly. Both Bantu and Tamara scouted all around them and twice they had to hide as bands of riding men raced to join up with the main force. Resson's army was growing. The one good thing about its swelling size was that the men had to camp early. It took time and daylight to set up the tents and start the evening fires.

Bantu found a secluded spot, sheltered behind a single huge boulder leaning against a hillside. The small cave it created was just big enough for Daniel and Jeanine to squeeze into with the two samkits next to them.

Jeanine wanted to go with Daniel, but he talked her out of it. She'd stay with Tamara while he and Bantu sneaked into the camp. If anything happened to him, he made her promise she'd stay with the samkits until she found Lauren. Bantu scouted ahead and found the roped-off area the guards had set up as a temporary prison. The large moon was only a sliver in the sky and the smaller circling one cast most of the moonlight. In the semidark sky, Daniel saw thousands of tiny stars over them. It looked very peaceful as he stared up. He wondered if somewhere, shining in the Lithian night sky, was his sun, his home. Then he thought about it and realized he was home.

Bantu could see very well, and soon Daniel crouched low behind a row of wild bushes growing near the cordoned area used as a jail. This wouldn't be easy. Unlike the sleeping guards who had watched Lauren, these men were wide awake. They carried swords and bows and constantly patrolled the jail's perimeter.

We have to get by them, thought Daniel. *We might be able to use Me if the guards stop and rest.*

Use Me? Me ready. Who Me spit? said Me from his pocket.

Not now, Me, thought Daniel. *I'll tell you when.* Once again he followed Bantu. They went to the far edge of the rope fence and watched a solitary guard walk back and forth, shaking his head to keep awake.

We will wait, said Bantu. *If he rests and puts the sword down, the wyerin can crawl onto its handle. The man will see and not move. Then you can approach him.*

They got as close as they could without being seen. Me was in Daniel's hand, ready to go. Daniel must have dozed off, for Bantu's nudge startled him. The guard was sitting, his sword resting on the ground.

Go, Me. Stay on the handle. If you lie on the blade he may not see you.

Me know, answered Me as it slipped away.

Now they watched. They moved closer to the resting man and waited. In a few minutes he shook his head, drank from his flask, and bent down to pick up his sword. Daniel heard Me's weak hissing in the eerie si-

116

lence of the night. The man froze. Daniel moved quickly. A twig broke beneath his feet, but the guard didn't look. When he stood next him, Daniel saw Me weaving back and forth, as if it were conducting an invisible orchestra. The wyerin was making sure the guard knew it was there.

Daniel whispered into the man's ear, "The wyerin obeys me."

What Me do? asked Me.

Just stay there, thought Daniel. He pulled the man's knife from his belt and continued talking. "The wyerin will open a hole in your head if you make a sound. Once they find you, they'll see what happened. They won't even search the area." Daniel picked Me up and told it to wrap itself around the man's wrist. "Come, and if you make one sound, you're dead."

The guard followed, walking very carefully and very quietly. When they were away from the roped area, Daniel used the man's belt and pants to tie him up. He cut a strip out of the man's shirt and stuffed it into his mouth just to make sure he wouldn't yell.

"I'm going to leave for a little while but the wyerin stays. If you move or try to escape, the wyerin will kill you. Understand?" The man nodded.

Daniel left, picking up the man's sword and leaving Me sitting on his naked leg. When he ducked under the rope, he saw the men sleeping, still tied to each other. He found the last man on one of the lines and woke him, putting his hand over the man's mouth to stop him from making any noise. "Shh," he whispered into the man's ear. When the man was fully awake, Daniel re-

117

moved his hand and cut the rope. "I'm here to help. Who's in charge?" he asked.

The man rose and silently made his way past the exhausted sleeping prisoners. He stopped and pointed when he found the man he was looking for. Daniel woke him, too. The man stared at him, not saying anything. Finally, he spoke. His whisper was cracked and hoarse. "I know you," he said. "From where?"

Daniel tried to recognize him, but the man's face was muddy and a dried blood-red bandage covered his forehead, trying to hide a space where an ear had once been attached. In the dim moonlight Daniel didn't know him. "I don't know," he said.

"What's your name?" asked the soldier.

"Daniel."

"Of course. The boy who rescued the queen. I met you briefly. I'm Tigert. It's no wonder you don't recognize me. How did you get here? How many men have you brought?"

"I'm alone," he answered. "I was trying to find Lauren when I ran into Resson's army. I couldn't leave without trying to do something. I don't have much. One sword and one knife. I don't know if they'll help, but . . . "

"They'll help," said Tigert. "And there's enough time for us tonight. Once we're free from these ropes . . . Tell me, how did you get . . . No, better not. I don't want to know." He took the knife and cut the ropes binding his neck and legs. Others were quietly awakened, and more men were freed. "You saved the queen once, and if we get away and warn her how close Resson is, you'll have saved her again. We . . ." He stopped for a second before continuing. "Will you come with us?"

Daniel wanted to say yes, but he didn't. He didn't know how the men would react if they knew they were traveling with Resson's daughter. "No, I can't. But if you could tell me where Lauren is, I could meet you there."

Tell Me what? Want Me spit?

No! Don't spit. Just stay there! Daniel's mind shouted. *Me, when this is over, I'm changing your name. I wasn't talking to you!*

No! No change. Me like Me, it said.

Tigert used the moment to think. "Daniel, Princess Lauren trusted you, and although you disappeared without a word, and some of her advisors thought you had something to do with the surprise attack the day after you came, she kept her trust in you. Resson seeks her, too. If I were to give you even a hint, and you were captured . . . you understand, don't you?" Tigert adjusted the bandage on his head and took a deep breath. Daniel didn't have to ask what happened to him.

"Okay," whispered Daniel. "We'll meet again, I hope."

Tigert grabbed his hand as he turned to leave. "When we do, I hope you'll tell me how you manage to pop up when you're needed. You saved many lives tonight."

Daniel smiled back. "Good luck."

"Be careful," he heard as he made his way back.

The guard was still there, in the same position. "I'm leaving now," Daniel said, picking Me up. Before he

119

left, he tied another strip of cloth around the man's mouth, sealing in the gag. Then he wrapped the man's hands and feet together with rope he had taken before leaving Tigert.

Go back to Tamara, said Bantu who was hiding behind the soldier. *Mount your horses and ride. You must be far away when they begin their escape. I will stay here and scout.*

But, how will we find you? Daniel asked.

Don't worry about me. I will not get lost. I will find you.

Why worry? Me not lost. Me not going. Me stay.

No, Me, thought Daniel as he walked back. *Bantu was talking to me, not you.*

Bantu no worry. Me no lost.

Go to sleep. I'll explain it to you later.

Daniel was met by Tamara, who led him the rest of the way. He woke Jeanine, but just as they were planning to leave, they heard shouts. Those shouts were followed by blaring trumpets and the sounds of horses running in all directions. The horses that Daniel and Jeanine held reared, frightened by the sudden noise. Before Daniel could calm them, they pulled their reins free, turned, and raced off. He and Jeanine were left standing alone, while the shouts of Resson's soldiers came closer and closer.

Chapter 11

For two days Daniel and Jeanine huddled together in the small cavelike shelter squeezed between the rock and the hillside, while Resson's men crisscrossed the entire area. They were searching for escaped prisoners and runaway horses. Whatever Tigert did, he did it well. Bantu reported the camp was in complete disarray. It took Resson most of the first day just to organize it. Tamara stayed with them, leaving only at night.

Bantu remained free, hiding among the rocks and trees, watching and telling Daniel what he saw. He appeared on the morning of the third day with news that Resson's forces had finally broken camp.

"Well," said Daniel, taking a good, long stretch, "we're out of food, have no horses, and are still a long way from Lauren. Are you up to walking?"

"We had no horses when we began," answered Jeanine. "We made out fine then, so I'm sure we'll do okay now. Besides, with all the animals that scattered, we might even find a horse or two." She knelt and gave Tamara a hug. "And they'll watch us. We don't have anything to worry about."

Daniel wanted to return the hug Jeanine was giving Tamara, but the samkit beat him to it. She licked Jeanine's face until Jeanine had enough and pushed her away.

They searched the campsite Resson's army used and found very little in the way of supplies. The only one able to make a meal of the leftovers was Me. The bits and pieces of fruit it found on the ground were more than enough for it.

They walked that day, following the tracks of Jeanine's father's army. Bantu and Tamara wove a net around them, constantly scouting on all sides. They paused briefly by an old fruit orchard, eating what they could and filling their empty saddle packs. At night, they pulled up grass to make the ground less hard.

Jeanine curled up, resting her head on the sleeping Tamara. Daniel didn't go to sleep right away. He sat up looking at the stars and watching the twin moons. When he turned back to Jeanine, he saw her fast asleep with her thumb securely planted in her mouth.

He smiled, thinking of his sister, Evelyn. She did that sometimes. When he had friends visiting him and she was being particularly obnoxious, he could get her to leave them alone by rubbing his thumb against his lips. Evelyn wanted everyone to think of her as an adult genius, and the thought of people knowing she sucked her thumb was so embarrassing that she would behave almost normally until Daniel's friends left. Funny, he thought. Deep down, he missed her. Maybe she wasn't such a brat after all. Maybe part of her brattiness was his fault. If he ever got home, he would behave differently toward her. "But it's too late now, isn't it, Evelyn," he whispered to the stars.

He looked at Jeanine again. Maybe when the war was over and Lauren was crowned queen, he would live with them in Bluecastle. Or, maybe he and Me would really go to Nivia. He just didn't know.

Tamara lifted her head when Bantu called. Her mate had made a kill and was calling her to eat. Daniel got up and took her place, putting Jeanine's head on his shoulder. He stroked Jeanine's hair, wiping strands away from her eyes and gently removing her thumb.

When he woke up, Jeanine, who had put her thumb back in her mouth, was still lying next to him. Bantu and Tamara were resting nearby. "Come on, sleepyhead," he said. "The sun's up, and we've a long way to go."

When Jeanine opened her eyes, she looked down and saw where her thumb was. She looked up and saw Daniel smiling at her. "If you ever tell, I'll . . . I'll do something terrible to you!"

He laughed. "Don't worry," he said, "I'm an old hand at keeping secrets, especially ones like yours. Here, have some fruit. Maybe Bantu can find us some water."

"All right," she answered. "Just remember, in case you ever tell, I know how to get revenge!"

During a stop for lunch, Bantu told them to hide behind some bushes. Coming toward them was a single soldier from Resson's army. Bantu had learned to recognize the shirts worn by each side. The soldier rode one horse and led another with heavy packs strapped to its back.

Daniel told Jeanine to stay with the samkits while he met the soldier. He'd take the horses and send the soldier on his way. Me would make sure there was no trouble. When Daniel stood up, the rider changed his course and headed toward him. Me was ready and poked his head out of his window.

There was something familiar about the rider. It wasn't until Daniel saw him clearly that he knew. "Artema!" he shouted, and ran the last few steps to meet him.

Artema looked startled for a second while he thought. Then a big smile appeared on his face. He jumped down and wrapped his arms around Daniel. "Of all the people in Lithia I could meet, I find the boy from Nivia. How are you, Daniel?"

The two sat on some rocks while the horses grazed. Jeanine and the samkits watched, remaining hidden.

"Where are you going?" asked Daniel.

"Home," he said. "I bought a little farm several years ago and thought this would be a good time to start living there." He pulled up some strands of grass and began tearing them into halves. "I once told you it made no difference who sat on the throne. I think I said if a few people suffer for the good of the rest, it was all right with me. Well, I was wrong. Since Resson left the capital and headed for Brata, I've seen too much. I used to think Resson did what he did because he had to. But now I'm not so sure. I think the man enjoys seeing others suffer, and I want no part in it. He's even recruiting farmers for his army whether they want to join or not. If those men aren't back home by harvest time, a lot of innocent people are going to be hungry this winter. No, Daniel, if I'm going to die, it won't be defending him. So I'm going home. Twenty-five years of soldiering is enough."

"Won't you get in trouble for deserting?"

"No one will miss me. The officers will just think I was killed."

"Why don't you join Lauren?" asked Daniel. "Then you could fight for something good, not evil."

"Like you?" he answered with a question of his own as he ran his hand along the dirty white stripe on Daniel's arm. "I'm too old for that, son. I'll be forty-seven next spring." He lifted his sword, raising it halfway out of its sheath. "It's been a long time since I used this in earnest. I'd be more of a liability than an asset. No, my place is back there. I'll leave the fighting to the younger ones. Come on, give me a hand with the packs."

"What do you mean?" asked Daniel.

"You don't think I'd leave you out here in the middle of nowhere, without anything but the clothes on your back, do you? We'll divide the supplies and I'll give you the pack horse. That way, you'll have a better chance of getting where you're going."

When everything was done, Artema stood and shook Daniel's hand. "I won't ask you where you're going or where you've been. You seem to be able to take care of yourself. I don't think we'll meet again, though. Be careful, son. You're a good lad and I'd hate for anything to happen to you."

"I will," answered Daniel. "And thanks."

Artema put one foot in the stirrup, but stopped before he hoisted himself up. "I don't suppose you'd let me see them?" he asked.

"Who?"

"Them."

"Them?" repeated Daniel.

Artema laughed. "Some things never change, do they, Daniel? The samkits, that's them. I never saw one, but I've heard they're really something."

"What makes you think I have a samkit?"

Artema put both feet on the ground and leaned on the saddle. "Rumors. When I was still in Bluecastle, a rider raced in yelling that Lauren had been captured. Did we ever celebrate that night, thinking the war was over! But Lauren never showed up. Instead, we heard that a boy with a pet wyerin frightened the guards and helped her escape. Next, a small company of soldiers was found with their captain's face missing. He obviously scared a wyerin. But the strange thing was that some of his men were torn apart by animals. No one really knew what happened. By this time, we're on our way here. A while ago we heard another story. This time someone claimed that not only did this boy have a wyerin, but he also had two samkits. Everyone knows samkits are extinct, so no one believed it. But now that I see you, it all makes sense. Remember, I saw you with the tamago."

Tamara, Bantu, Daniel thought. *You can come out. This man is my friend. He won't tell anyone about you.*

Artema looked up when he heard the bushes rustle. He watched as the samkits came out, but when he saw Jeanine with them he dropped to one knee. "Your Highness!" When he got up and walked to her, Daniel followed. "They really are beautiful, aren't they, Princess? Just goes to show you how foolish people are. How could anyone hunt beasts like this? It seems you've found some good friends to watch over you. I'm glad. You've always needed someone."

"Aren't you surprised to see me, Artema?" she said.

"Nothing surprises me anymore. Take care of those animals, miss. After the war they can have kittens. Who knows, in a hundred years, maybe everyone will be able to see how beautiful they are. Thank you, Daniel," he said. "I'll tell my children about this, if I ever have any. You'd better help me again. I can't ride off knowing Jeanine's with you. You take both horses. I'll carry what I need."

"Thank you, Artema," said Jeanine, "but you don't have to. We'll make out fine with the one you gave Daniel. I'll remember your kindness when we meet again."

Artema leaned over and hugged her, kissing her when he parted. "Don't tell your father I did that. He'd kill me for kissing the heir to the throne. You take care of her, Daniel. She's one special lady."

Jeanine began to blush so Artema turned back to his horse. "You're a strange lad, Daniel," he said. "If I were twenty years younger, I'd join you." As he mounted, Jeanine came to stand next to Daniel. "One last thing," Artema said. "Do you really have a wyerin? Or was that just a trick?"

Daniel reached into his pocket and pulled Me out. "It's real."

"Well, I'll be," said Artema.

"Thank you again," said Jeanine.

"Be careful, you two. Imagine, samkits and tame wyerins! What's this world coming to! Next thing I'll hear is that you found those wizards you were asking people about." He shook his head and laughed to himself as he rode away.

" 'Bye," yelled Jeanine after him. She stayed next to Daniel, watching Artema get smaller and smaller as he moved farther and farther away.

"What wizards?" asked Jeanine.

"I figured that if there were people who could do magic, they might be able to send me home."

Jeanine leaned against him. "I'm glad there aren't any. I'm glad you're here."

Daniel put an arm around her shoulder as they watched Artema disappear. "Come on, let's go," he finally said. They traveled quickly now, resting only when the horse was tired. Sometimes they both rode. Sometimes they both walked. They saw no one, hiding whenever one of the samkits saw riders moving to join Resson's main army.

"How are we going to find Laurie?" asked Jeanine during one of their rest stops.

"We're not," answered Daniel. "We're going to let your father do it for us. Lauren must know he's here

128

and is massing his army for an attack. She has to be doing the same. We can follow Resson's trail until he camps. Then, with Bantu's help, we'll sneak around his army and into Lauren's camp."

"That plan is as good as any," she said. "Besides, Father's heading in the same direction as Mirror Lake. As long as we aren't seen, we might as well tag along."

Later that day Tamara called Daniel. She had disappeared into a small forest of trees that poked their heads over the fields of the neighboring countryside. He tied the horse, and with Jeanine walking behind, entered the tiny woods.

Quietly, said Tamara as they came next to her. Within the trees, there was a tiny meadow. In one corner of the pasture three mighty mahemuths were peacefully eating.

"Wow!" said Jeanine. "Do you think one of them is Hira? Do you think she'd help you again?"

"Only one way to find out," he answered. He stood up and walked into the open so the mahemuths could see him.

"Hira," he called out. "Is that you?"

Instantly, the heads of the mahemuths shot up. They turned, and, lining up next to each other, charged straight at him.

Chapter 12

For a moment, Daniel knew the same fear the soldiers who met Me felt. The three mahemuths loomed before him. Their pounding hooves came closer and closer. He could sense their hearts beating as they ran.

He was knocked aside by Bantu and Tamara. The two samkits stood before him, roaring and preparing to leap. Their teeth flashed in the sun as they crouched low, ready to spring. Jeanine ran behind Daniel. Even Me felt the fear and restlessly moved inside his pocket.

But Daniel came to his senses. He blinked and stepped in front of the snarling samkits. *Stop!* he thought. *We mean you no harm. Please, don't force the samkits to attack. Stop!*

The mahemuths were only twenty feet away when one of them whinnied and began to slow. When it stopped, the others did also. The mahemuths' nostrils flared. They pawed the ground, daring the samkits to jump. They weren't afraid.

Daniel turned his back and spoke with the samkits. "It's okay," he said, petting Tamara. Her hair was all bristled, her ears pulled back. "They won't hurt us. Calm down." He turned and stroked Bantu, trying to push his fur back into place. When he was satisfied the cats were no longer angry, he walked to the mahemuths. He was sure the one on the left was Hira.

Hira, it's me, Daniel. Don't you remember?

Me know you. You silly. Me no forget.

No, Me, not you, Hira, answered Daniel.

The black mare lowered her head and stared at him. Daniel saw the fire in her eyes and felt her remembering. She snorted and lowered her head so Daniel could reach up and hug her.

This is Bantu and Tamara, he thought. *They are friends.*

I see their kind before. Attack young ones.

They won't hurt you. They are with m . . . They seek the same one I do. We are traveling together.

The mahemuth stepped toward them. Her head went down and touched the outstretched nose of Bantu. When each was sure the other posed no threat, they broke away.

Did you understand what she said? Daniel thought to Bantu.

I heard only you.

That's funny. You can talk to M . . . to the wyerin but not to any other animal. I wonder why? He looked back at Hira. *Hira, I need your help again. I know I've no claim on you, nor do I even have a right to ask, but I must find Lauren. With your speed, we could find her*

131

more easily. Would you let us ride you? I wouldn't ask except it's important.

Hira looked to the two mahemuths standing behind her. She snorted, and they moved away. Then they took off, throwing clods of grass their feet ripped up behind them.

I help, said Hira.

That's great! thought Daniel. *Thanks.*

He felt a gentle tug on his shirt. "What was that all about?" she asked. "Is this the mahemuth you let go?"

Daniel realized the entire conversation was done in mind-speech, and all Jeanine had heard was a tension-filled silence.

"Yes. This is Hira, and she's going to help us. She said I could ride her."

"Oh," answered Jeanine. She turned away and began walking back to the horse. Her head was down, and she looked like a puppy who had been scolded by its owner.

Daniel didn't understand why she felt so bad, but when Hira pushed against his chest, he knew. He ran after her. "You think I'm going to ride Hira while you ride the horse, don't you?"

She nodded.

"Don't be ridiculous," he said. "We're both going to ride her. If you rode the other one, we'd have to wait for you all the time. Hira can carry both of us."

Now her face lit up. She hugged Daniel hard, and it made him feel good inside. When she stepped away she jumped up, clapping her hands together. "I get to ride a mahemuth," she shouted. "I get to ride a mahemuth!"

Suddenly Daniel felt a little sorry for her. In an im-

132

portant way, she and Evelyn were very similar. Neither was an average girl. Jeanine was Resson's daughter, a princess, and even before this war started, that must have been a heavy responsibility. He wondered if she had friends her own age, if being a princess had taken all the fun out of growing up. He knew being a genius had taken the fun out of Evelyn's childhood.

"Come on," he said. "I'll race you to the horse." She took off with the samkits right behind her. Daniel made sure she won. Once they had transferred the saddle and travel packs, they began. By the next day they had caught up with the tail end of Resson's army.

"This is no good," said Daniel. "We can't follow them this closely; we're bound to be seen eventually. With Hira's speed, we can circle them during the night and be far away by dawn. Jeanine, do you still think Lauren is in the Valley of Mirror Lake?"

"I'm not sure, but it makes sense, doesn't it?"

"All right. We'll head straight for it. If she's not there, we'll backtrack until we find your father's army and continue to follow him. Do you know the way?"

"I think so. It's in the Terdas Mountains."

The scenery didn't change as they headed toward the hidden valley. It remained the same, small hills connected by long patches of flat land. But as they traveled, the lands became more populated than those they just came from. Farmers cut deeply into the soil with their plows. Villages sprang up like daisies in a field. Bantu and Tamara wove a crooked path, avoiding working farmers and the houses their families lived in. But they always returned to face the tall mountains pointing their snow-covered tops toward the summer sun.

When they found a huge lake the following day, Jeanine knew they were headed in the right direction. Bantu kept them far away from the water because he saw a large village. People in small boats were fishing in the crystal-clear water while women stayed on the shore cleaning the fish their men caught. Children splashed in the shallows, laughing and playing.

As they moved farther from the village, Jeanine began to squirm in the saddle. "What's bothering you?" asked Daniel. "You're acting as if you're sitting on an anthill."

"I know," she said, "I'm itchy! I want to go swimming. Do you think Bantu could find a place where there aren't any people?"

"That's not a good idea," said Daniel. "We've been very lucky to steer clear of any soldiers, and the closer we get to Mirror Lake, the harder it will become. We don't have the time."

"No!" shouted Jeanine, as she swung her leg over Hira's neck and jumped down. "I'm not going! I'm going to sit down, and I'm not moving until you say yes!" Jeanine plopped herself on the ground and vigorously rubbed her fingers back and forth on her head. "I itch!" she yelled. "And if you try to make me leave without going in the water first, I'll scream so loud my father will hear me wherever he is!"

Daniel let out a deep breath. Then he told Bantu what Jeanine had said. The samkit walked over to her, put his face next to hers, pulled his lips back, and growled.

Jeanine crossed her arms over her chest, looked him

straight in the eye, and growled right back at him. "Tell Bantu," she said, "that I've got him pegged. He's nothing more than a big pussycat. He won't hurt me. He likes me, and I know it!"

Daniel found it hard to keep a straight face, but he did. He told Bantu. Bantu turned quickly, making sure his tail slapped against Jeanine. *Cubs!* he said.

"You win," said Daniel. "Come on."

Bantu found the quiet beach Jeanine hoped for, but neither he nor Tamara went in the water. They were too close to populated areas to risk being caught off guard. The samkits watched and waited while Jeanine and Daniel scrubbed themselves clean with sand.

"Daniel," said Jeanine after they began traveling again, "do you still like me?" Daniel refused to answer.

They followed the crooked shoreline for the rest of the day and half of the next. They often had to leave the lake altogether in order not to be seen. It was late in the afternoon when they finally reached the end of the lake.

Now Jeanine became excited; she recognized the land Hira traveled over very well. She pointed to a formation of rocks that jutted out of a farm field. She told Daniel that the last time she had come this way she had ridden in a coachlike wagon. She had had to ride inside, not being allowed to sit next to the driver. Since she had no companions, she had entertained herself by making up stories. The rocks they just passed had become a dragon. She laughed and told him of the imaginary battle she had fought in that very spot. "I won," she said.

"That's why the dragon will never fly again. I killed its magic."

At the next landmark she pointed out, she said, "Four days. That's how long it took us to reach Neus from here. That's the city near the valley we're looking for. Since we can move much faster on Hira, it shouldn't take us that long. I only hope Lauren is really there."

Jeanine was wrong. It didn't take four days to reach the mountain. It took almost eight. The land was alive with people: soldiers were everywhere. The closer they got to the Terdas Mountains, the more often they had to hide. Soldiers dressed in brown and gray raced past them from all directions. Both samkits ranged farther ahead than ever, warning Daniel not to follow until they found a place for Hira to hide. They leapfrogged from one hiding place to the next. The last part of their journey was fast becoming the most dangerous.

"Lauren must be in the valley," he told Jeanine, "and I'm sure your father knows it. It's not just a coincidence everyone is going the same way."

Bantu and Tamara were their guardian angels. They made sure that when the mahemuth ran, no one was near. It seemed as though they would be riding and hiding forever, but finally they reached their goal. With Hira well hidden, Daniel and Jeanine crawled to a high, flat rock that allowed them to see far off in the distance. They were on the edge of a high ridge that stood guard over a wide valley floor teeming with activity. Tents were everywhere, and more were being set up as additional men poured into the valley from all directions.

Huge herds of horses were corralled in several areas, and smoke from countless fires filled the air. This was Resson's main army, numbering well into the thousands.

"There," said Jeanine, pointing to a gap in the mountain wall directly opposite them. "That's the entrance to the hidden valley. Mirror Lake is through that opening. Lauren must be there."

"With all these soldiers, it's a miracle your father hasn't attacked yet," he said.

"He can't. I told you the passageway through the mountain is very narrow."

"Well, narrow or not, we've got to get in. "Do you think we could climb over the sides and reach the valley that way?"

"No. I don't even think Bantu and Tamara could climb it. The walls are too steep. That was one reason Lauren loved this place. With a few guards in the alleyway, she could have the entire valley to herself."

They crawled back while Bantu left to see if he could find another way in. He didn't return until the sun was down and the sky was dotted by millions of tiny lights.

It is as she said. There is no way for you and her. Tamara and I can find a way in, but you could never follow. The only way is through the opening.

We'll have to sneak in, thought Daniel. *Hira can carry us around the army's guards, letting us off next to the side of the mountain. We'll walk the rest of the way on foot.*

It is the only way, said Bantu. *But it will be dangerous.*

Daniel told Jeanine what Bantu had discovered. She agreed with his plan. It was the only one that made any sense. Then he spoke with Hira. He felt rather small as he silently stood next to the large mahemuth. Her red eyes stared down at him while he spoke.

I help. I no leave. I carry you.

But you'll be trapped. There's no way out of the valley except the way we go in. I don't want you captured again. I don't want Resson to ever sit on your back.

The dark mare lowered her head and pushed lightly against his chest. *You ask help,* she said. *I help.*

Daniel wrapped his arms around her face, pressing his cheek next to the baby-soft skin of her nose. "Thank you," he whispered. Together with Bantu, they decided. They'd do as Daniel suggested, only once they reached the side of the mountain, Hira would make a dash for the opening. With her great speed, they should be inside before anyone blocked their path. They'd leave right before sunrise, after the guards had spent most of the night trying to stay awake.

Daniel and Jeanine slept while they waited; Tamara woke them up when it was time to leave. They left their safe hiding place and headed around a sea of sleeping men. They passed the perimeter of Resson's camp unnoticed, swinging wide so the guards wouldn't see them. Daniel hardly heard Hira's hooves. The massive animal was being as cautious as a mouse sneaking past a sleeping cat.

When they reached the area for Hira's race, a half mile or more before the opening, the samkits left. They couldn't keep up with a mahemuth running at full speed. They needed a head start if they hoped to enter the passageway at the same time as Daniel.

Daniel sat, waiting for Bantu's signal, arms wrapped around Jeanine's waist. His stomach began to roll over. "Hang on tightly," he whispered. She nodded and leaned forward, wrapping her hands in Hira's mane. He bent low, pushing her farther down into the mahemuth's back. When he heard Bantu's call, he spoke softly into Hira's ear. "Let's go."

Hira began from a statue-still pose to a moving mountain of fury racing at top speed. The wind howled past Daniel's ears, and the sudden burst of speed almost threw him to the ground. Hira had run with them before, but never like this. The once silent steps of the mahemuth now echoed in the early light. Men shouted and trumpets cracked the stillness of the dawn. Daniel looked up as they neared the opening. Two white blurs disappeared into the valley entrance.

Arrows flew over his head, whistling in anger at missing their targets. Horses were beginning to race after them, but he didn't look back.

"We're almost there," he shouted. "Come on, Hira! Show them what you can do!"

There was only one barrier left. Four men on horseback, swords flashing in the ever-growing light. They stood their ground before the opening.

"Stop!" yelled one of them. "In the name of the king, I order you to stop!"

Daniel leaned down, pushing the air out of Jeanine's lungs but keeping his chest slightly raised so he wouldn't hurt Me. "Hang on!" The mahemuth never slowed. The four horses began to move nervously from side to side. The men had to lower their swords to keep them steady. Daniel had an idea. He visualized the samkits, crouching low, fangs out, ready to jump. He sent this image to the minds of the horses. They reared and bolted, carrying their cursing masters with them.

While arrows still flew over them, Hira raced into the opening. The shouts of the pursuing soldiers faded into the distance. For a brief moment Daniel heard only Hira's heavy breathing and the pounding of her feet. Then he heard other noises; shouts and screams, horses running, and horns sounding. These new sounds didn't come from behind. These were made by men and animals in front. Hira burst into the valley, just as riders wearing the green and white galloped past her, daring Resson's troops to continue chasing the mahemuth.

Hira decreased her speed, and by the time she reached Lauren's camp, she was walking. Daniel and Jeanine sat erect in the saddle, and the samkits trotted next to them.

Hira stopped when a small band of men blocked their path. Each held a sword as they stared unbelievingly from the giant mahemuth to the two samkits who sat by her side. Daniel jumped off, leaving Jeanine alone in the saddle. The samkits moved closer to him. For the first time since he met them, he sensed fear. They were afraid.

"These are friends of mine," he said resting his hands on Tamara's neck. "Your swords are frightening them." The soldiers didn't move. Even though they were standing, some were just beginning to realize they were not dreaming.

"Didn't you hear what he said?" shouted a voice. "Put away those swords!" Pushing his way through the ever-enlarging crowd, Daniel saw a one-eared man approaching.

"Captain Tigert?" he asked.

"Hello, Daniel. I see you found your way after all. And seeing the companions you travel with, I understand how you made it. You recruited the mahemuth again, too." Now his gaze went to Jeanine, whose hair had fallen in front of her face. "You have another friend. Let me help her down." He walked to Hira, passing within inches of Tamara. He showed no fear of the samkit.

Daniel became tense. He didn't know what Tigert's reaction would be when he found out who his friend was.

Tigert stopped a foot away from the mahemuth. He peeked up. "Jeanine?" he said in a half whisper. "We heard you were dead. Is it really you?"

Her head bobbed up and down as she parted her hair. "Hello, Ti," she said.

"Jeanine!" he yelled as he lifted her off and wrapped his arms around her. "I thought you were dead. Give thanks to the Creator you aren't."

Jeanine didn't answer. Her head was buried deep in his shoulders and her arms clung around his neck. When Tigert turned to Daniel, his eyes were as misty as Jeanine's. "Thank you, Daniel."

"We have to talk, Daniel," said a soft voice from behind. Turning, Daniel saw Lauren, who was as beautiful as he remembered.

When Tigert finally put Jeanine down, she walked

141

toward Lauren. "Hi, Laurie," she said. "Are you angry with me?"

Lauren laughed as she knelt down and opened her arms to catch the running child. When she stood up, she grabbed Jeanine under her arms and swung her in a wide circle, making several soldiers jump back. "Don't be silly. You haven't done anything to me yet. You just got here!"

"No," said Jeanine. "I mean about what my father's done."

"I love you," said Lauren, "and nothing Resson does will ever change that." When Jeanine started crying, Lauren laughed and smoothed her hair, whispering that she was safe, and everything would be all right. Daniel, too, had to wipe his eyes. Whatever fears he had for Jeanine's safety were gone. The little princess had found people to love and care for her. Tigert came and stood next to him.

"Jeanine's mother died when she was born," he said. "I think Resson blamed her because he never spent much time watching her grow. He always sent her to relatives and managed to find some excuse for not visiting. Jeanine spent more time with Lauren and me than with him. I love her just as much as I do my own daughter."

"Then she'll be cared for when this is over?" asked Daniel.

"Like the princess she is," answered Tigert, putting his arm on Daniel's shoulder. "Come," he said following Lauren and Jeanine. "There's no more time for secrets, and I'm very curious to hear your story."

The crowding soldiers scattered like blowing sand, giving Daniel and Tigert, who were flanked by Tamara and Bantu, all the room they needed.

Chapter 13

The talk Lauren asked for lasted several hours. Present besides Daniel and Jeanine were the two samkits, Captain Tigert, and a man Lauren introduced as General Maston. He had been her mother's leading adviser, and when the uprising began, Lauren asked him to lead her forces.

The meeting was difficult for Daniel and he soon tired. He had to repeat, in mind-speech, everything everyone said so the samkits could understand. In the beginning, it was easy. He told the story just as he told Jeanine. The only thing he left out was the communication the samkits had with each other.

Whenever Maston or Tigert interrupted, Daniel translated for the samkits. Most of the interruptions were questions about Daniel's past. At first, they didn't believe he was from another world. They finally believed after realizing that the boy sitting next to them was talking to two samkits just as easily as they were

143

talking to him. Maston knew Empaths could transmit feelings to animals. But even an accomplished Empath could not talk to them as easily as Daniel did. Then they wanted to know how he got to their world. Tamara and Bantu were silent as everyone offered opinions on how and why Daniel appeared. None of the ideas made any sense.

When Daniel finished his story, Jeanine spoke, adding whatever she thought Daniel had left out. And finally, when the last question had been asked and answered, Daniel sat back and wiped his forehead with his sleeve. Jeanine had left her chair a long while before, choosing to sit on the floor between the samkits. She would pet Tamara occasionally, scratching the samkit behind her ear. Tamara would begin to purr, and the sound would cause everyone to stop talking. Jeanine would stop and smile at them. The discussion would continue until the next time Jeanine got bored and started petting Tamara again.

Lauren called for a scribe, who cautiously walked around the lying animals. She told the scribe to write down a new law. Any person who hunted, killed, or in any way injured a samkit would be exiled from Lithia.

"Tell the samkits what I've done," she said to Daniel. "But tell them also that the only way for it to become a law will be for us to defeat Resson."

"They know that already."

Me want, too! Daniel heard.

"What?" Daniel said aloud. "What do you want?" Everyone turned to him as he pulled Me from his pocket. No one had overreacted when Daniel told them how he met Me, but seeing the wyerin was a different

144

story. Everyone backed away. But when they saw Lauren lean toward the wyerin in Daniel's hand, they returned to their seats.

"Tell Me I can't make a law forbidding people to step on wyerins. No one wants to step on them. And besides, their poison is far worse than any punishment I could impose."

Daniel told Me, word for word, what Lauren had said. Me rose up in Daniel's hand to look at the princess. It moved its head back and forth, looking from Daniel to Lauren. Daniel heard no answer, but for some inexplicable reason, he felt himself becoming warm. *Me, are you embarrassed?* Me didn't answer. It left his hand and began traveling along his arm, across his chest, and dropped into his pocket.

Me no want law. Me hungry.

Daniel laughed. "Me doesn't want a law. It wants something to eat."

Lauren smiled and picked up a large orange-colored fruit. She held it near the window in Daniel's pocket. Me stuck its head out of the opening. Its tongue moved slowly. *Too big,* it said to Daniel and went back to hide.

When Daniel told Lauren, the princess looked at her scribe. "Can you get something smaller for Daniel's friend?" she asked. The man tripped over a chair in his effort to make a hasty retreat. He returned within a minute, carrying a tray of small fruit. But he didn't give the tray to Lauren. He cautiously placed it on the table and backed away. Dealing with samkits was one thing. Being friends with a wyerin was a completely different matter.

Daniel took Me out of his pocket and put it on the

table. It slithered to the tray, picked the pieces of fruit it wanted, and ate them. No one spoke while Me ate. When it told Daniel it was finished, he picked it up and put it back into his pocket.

Tell thank you, it said as it coiled up to take a nap.

"I can accept many things," said General Maston, who had stood picture-still while Me was eating, "but if I live to be a thousand, I'll never get over seeing that!"

"Yes, you will," answered Tigert. "Whom are you going to tell it to? No one will believe it." He laughed with Maston.

"What happens now?" asked Daniel.

"As you can guess, we are trapped here," said General Maston. "Resson has over fifteen thousand soldiers outside, and we have about five. We weren't ready for this major battle, but we didn't have a choice, either. Resson surprised us with his large army and we just made it here hours before he arrived. For the moment, there's a stalemate. He can't attack us, and we can't attack him."

Jeanine yawned.

"You're tired," said Lauren. "A tent has been set up behind this one. Daniel, you and Jeanine may share it with your samkits and pocket friend."

After resting, changing clothes, and eating, and while Jeanine and Tamara wandered through the camp, Daniel sat alone with Bantu. They found a secluded place away from the noise and stares of Lauren's men.

"Bantu, you know if Lauren loses, and Resson becomes king, her law will not stand."

I know. We had a bargain. We knew the odds when

146

we began. You did your part, and Lauren did as you asked. Whatever the outcome, you have nothing to be sorry for.

"You and Tamara have done a lot for your clans. You risked your lives so they may be free. Are there others who would do as you did?"

I do not understand.

"I probably shouldn't ask, but can you help Lauren?"

What can I do? said Bantu. *I can frighten many men. But there are thousands out there, and two samkits will not make them go away.*

"Not two, but two hundred, two thousand. They might make a difference. Aren't there other samkits who would fight for this chance? Are there any samkits who live near here that you could speak to?"

You think I can enlist the aid of the clans? asked Bantu.

"I hope so. It's their fight just as much as Lauren's. If Lauren wins, they win, too, and they will finally escape from exile in the mountains. For generations to come, their children will be free to roam wherever they want."

I do not know. There is much hatred between my kind and yours.

"It's worth a try," said Daniel. "We can't lose anything if they say no. And there is another reason." Bantu sat still, waiting for Daniel to continue. "If Resson does attack, I don't want you and Tamara here. You said it yourself. There is nothing you can do. I'd like to think of you safe with your cubs."

Bantu arched his back and put his front legs far in front of him as he stretched. He looked over the evening

147

campfires. It was very peaceful in this camp of war. *We will go,* he said. *Do not expect us to return with an army. There are clans who live near here. If they will listen and help, we have ways of reaching our brothers in far places. It will take time.*

"How long?" asked Daniel.

I don't know. The samkit looked at the sky. *The sun goes. It may have to do that fifteen times before we return.*

"Thanks," said Daniel. "I know you don't like to be petted, but . . . " He put his arms around Bantu and gave the large cat a hug. "If, when you return, you see Resson is within the valley, don't . . ."

We will not enter.

"Good," said Daniel.

Let us see if the clans will fight for their birthright, said the samkit. Daniel heard him call Tamara and watched as the animals disappeared into the surrounding hills.

When he returned to his tent he found Jeanine, eyes red from crying. It made him think of Hira. He wanted to make sure the place Tigert set aside for the mahemuth to graze wasn't overly crowded with curious soldiers.

Jeanine told him Tamara had gone. She had seen her run into the hills with Bantu. "Will they come back?" she asked.

"Maybe," he said. "I have to talk to you about them, in case they do." He stopped, not knowing exactly what to say. He could see Jeanine was upset and didn't want to upset her more, but it couldn't be helped. "Jeanine, Bantu and Tamara were born without any masters ex-

148

cept their own will. They stayed with us because they wanted to, not because they had to. I don't know if you'll ever see them again, but if you do, you must be prepared to lose them forever."

"But if I . . ."

Daniel interrupted her. "No buts. You can never put a leash on them and keep them as house pets. You can never put them in a cage so you can see them when you want to. What you want doesn't count. What they want does. They are free, and they decide where they go and whom they stay with. That's the reason they came into this camp, to make sure their children don't have to hide every time they smell a human. I want your word on this, Jeanine. Not the word of a spoiled girl who is very good at getting people to do what she wants. I want the word of a princess who understands the meaning of honor."

Jeanine let out a deep breath. "I know," she said. "I promise. Never anything except what they want. Okay?"

"That's my sister!" he said. "Now, I've got to check on Hira. Then, I'm off to find Maston."

"Can I come?" she asked.

Daniel looked at her, and instantly thought of Evelyn. She must have asked him that a thousand times, and most of the time he answered no. If only he could go back. If only he could talk to her once more. "Of course you can," he said. "I'm sure Hira would love to see you."

Jeanine went to sleep early that night, and Daniel set out to find Maston. When he was told the general was with Princess Lauren, he asked the guard to tell them he would like to see them. He was soon escorted into

the same room where Jeanine and he had been questioned. Lauren looked tired. There were lines deeply
etched under her eyes, and her eyelids kept closing.

"How long do you think before Resson tries to push
into the valley?" he asked.

"A few days, maybe a little more. It's hard to tell,"
answered Maston. "He's getting impatient. He can't be
officially declared regent-ruler until Lauren is either
dead or convicted and dethroned."

"I need two weeks," said Daniel. "Can you think of
something that will delay him that long?"

"Maybe, but why?" asked Maston. "In two weeks
he'll have more men, and we'll have the same number.
What possible difference can two weeks make?"

"I can't tell you," answered Daniel. To answer it
would mean he'd have to break his promise to Bantu's
people about their mind-speaking to each other. "I'm
not saying in two weeks some miracle will happen, and
we'll be able to defeat Resson. I'm saying if we wait,
we might have an easier time when the fighting starts.
Please don't ask for any details. I can't give them."

Lauren stood up. "I am sorry, but I'm dead tired. I
can't think straight anymore." She looked at Maston.
"Think of something that will do what Daniel wants. I
trust him."

Maston stood at attention. "I will try, Your
Highness."

Daniel thanked Lauren, turned, and left. A few
minutes later, he was fast asleep. He slept deep and
long, not waking until well past noon, when the blaring
of horns and the shouts of men invaded his tent.

"To horse!" he heard.

"Get your swords!" yelled another.

He ran out and stopped the first soldier he saw. "What's happening?"

"Resson. He's preparing to attack!"

Daniel headed for Hira. He didn't know what he could do, but he would do whatever he could to get the mahemuth out of the trapped valley.

Men were everywhere as he left the shadow of his tent and stepped into the sunlight. He heard his name being shouted and looked up. He saw Jeanine waving at him, motioning for him to join her. She was standing next to Lauren. He had to look twice because she no longer had on the drab peasant dress she had worn since he met her. She had changed into a skirt made of several shades of gray cloth. Woven throughout the material were gold threads that picked up the sun's rays and threw them into his eyes. Her blouse was white with a green design embroidered over her chest. It was the same design flying on the flag over Lauren's tent.

"You look beautiful!" he said. Jeanine lowered her eyes and pushed her head into Lauren's side.

"Where were you going?" asked Lauren.

"To get Hira. If Resson is attacking, I want to help."

"If Daniel helps, I want to, too!" said Jeanine.

"What can either of you do?" asked Lauren. "Soldiers are trained to fight, you're not. Besides, if you sat on Hira, you'd be an easy target. Let her stay where she is, unbridled. If Resson manages to get into the valley, she'll have a better chance of escaping without any reins on her."

"Can I at least bring Hira here?" asked Jeanine.

"No," said Lauren. "I'm not asking you, Jeanine, I'm telling you. You and Daniel are staying here!"

Jeanine pulled away and put her hands on her hips. Just as she opened her mouth, Daniel coughed. When Jeanine looked at him, he was rubbing his lower lip with his thumb. Jeanine glared at him, but he just smiled back. The glare turned into a smile, and she walked over to him.

"Daniel, if Resson does get in the valley, I want you to do something," said Lauren.

"Whatever I can," he answered.

"Take Jeanine and hide in the mountains. After Resson leaves, take her with you out of Lithia. I've never been to Nivia, but I've heard it's a nice place."

Daniel nodded, but didn't look at her. He took a deep breath and waited. General Maston galloped toward them, pulling hard on the reins to bring his horse to a quick, full stop. "Everything is ready," he shouted. "I've had the men working all night to buy Daniel the time he wanted. We have only to wait." Lauren waved, and he vanished into the crowd of moving men.

Daniel watched the soldiers spread out. Archers stood, with quivers full and arrows notched, on both sides of the passage opening. Horseman lined up behind them, each with a lance held ready for the charge. They formed a large, tight semicircle, and the horses pawed the ground, waiting to run. Behind them was the rest of Lauren's army.

"What's Resson going to do?" asked Daniel.

"He's lining up his troops," answered Lauren, "three

abreast, before the entrance. His men will charge. He hopes that the large numbers of men he has will force my soldiers back into the valley. Once that happens, the rest of his army can enter. As long as we hold the entranceway, it's the only strategy he can use."

It was almost as though Resson were listening to her. The muffled sound of trumpets coming from beyond the passage announced the start of the battle.

"It's beginning," said Lauren, more to herself than to Daniel or Jeanine.

Soon the first of Resson's cavalry appeared, driving Lauren's men back. Resson's soldiers rode at full speed, bodies bent low, swords held tightly against their horses' necks. The air twanged with the sound of flying arrows. Men and horses fell. Daniel gasped. Pain, dull and sharp, gnawing and stabbing, entered his body. His legs buckled, his eyes watered. He watched horses with arrows sticking out of their necks and sides fall. Some tried to rise while others were trampled by the horses who still poured into the opening. The pain grew. He grabbed Lauren and dug his fingers into her arm for support.

"You feel the pain of the animals?" she asked. He looked at her, but couldn't get his mouth to answer.

By now, the head of Resson's army was past the archers and saw the pointed lances of Lauren's horsemen racing toward them. Behind those horses, the rest of Lauren's army surged forward. They fought like wild animals, not giving up an inch of ground until the weight of the advancing line pushed too hard for them to withstand. And still more men, fresh and eager to fight, entered the hidden valley. It was not going well.

Daniel heard a high-pitched trumpet ringing over the sound of the battle. It was followed by another noise, a low rumbling sound that grew louder with each passing second. Even the fighters heard it and many stopped to look toward the passageway. Lauren's men raced back twenty or thirty feet to regroup, and Resson's army didn't press them. Their faces were looking behind them. Dust was thrown into the air when everyone heard a final crash. Daniel fainted.

When he opened his eyes, the battle had stopped. Soldiers on both sides were milling around, looking to their officers for orders. From his lying position, he heard Maston's voice.

"Listen to me before you die foolishly. We have sealed the opening behind you. Tons of rocks bury those who waited to join this battle, and those who were outside have nowhere to ride. Put up your weapons. By the order of Princess Lauren, no one who does as I ask shall be harmed."

There was a long silence. Resson's men stared at the now settling dust still clogging the air behind them. A sword was dropped, then a second fell, and a third. The rest came too quickly to count.

Daniel was helped to his feet, and he saw Maston come. "We've won a small victory," the general said. "You have your two weeks, son. It'll take Resson at least that long to clear the passage. The avalanche sealed it."

Daniel couldn't answer. He didn't protest when Lauren led him away and laid him down on his bed. His eyes closed, and he slept.

Chapter 14

Maston's plan gave Daniel more than the two weeks he asked for. It gave him more than three. The general ordered his men to scale the heights that overlooked the blockage, and from positions too high for arrows to reach, they hurled rocks down on Resson's work force. They did very little damage, rarely hitting anyone. But with each rumbling sound, Resson's men scurried for cover. It was a delaying tactic, and while there were boulders to loosen, it worked. However, after six days, the clearing of the passageway went unhindered.

Lauren's men were relaxed. They swam, practiced with their weapons, or lay bare-chested in the sun. Until the rocks were removed, they were safe.

Lauren and Jeanine went among the prisoners shortly after the valley was closed. Hearing Jeanine speak against her father, and listening to Lauren, made many of them think about who really killed the former queen. After a day, more than half of them asked to trade their brown shirts for green ones. The rest were released. They were brought to the lowest possible place that overlooked the work teams. A truce was called, and the men were lowered on long ropes. Maston didn't know how long they would be trapped in the valley and didn't want to waste their food on prisoners. Killing them was out of the question.

Daniel began to worry as the second week drew to a close. Bantu should have been back. He hoped his friends were safe. It was early evening on the twentieth day when Daniel heard startled shouts from the rear of the camp. The samkits had returned. They had obviously found a way through the mountains. He ran out of his tent in time to see Jeanine being tackled by Tamara. The little princess laughed and giggled as the large samkit purred and licked her face raw. Bantu waited near them, and let Jeanine hug and kiss him, too. When Jeanine finished, Bantu went to Daniel.

"You've come back," said Daniel. "I'm glad you're all right."

It took us longer than we expected. We, too, are glad you are here, unhurt.

"Did the clans believe you? Did they agree to help?"

Some. Many others prepare to flee the land entirely.

"How many samkits came with you?" asked Daniel.

Five hundred or so. Most are young, without mates or cubs. They are eager to repay your kind for the hurt they have caused us. They wait beyond, but I do not know how such a small number can turn the tide of the battle.

Daniel sat and rubbed the samkit behind his ear. "Come on," he said. "Let's find Maston."

Later, in Lauren's tent, Maston sat staring at the two samkits. He remained silent, and when he spoke, he didn't move his eyes from Daniel. "If I understand you correctly, there are over five hundred samkits out there who will do what you tell them."

"That's right," answered Daniel. "That's why I needed the extra time. Bantu and Tamara had to find them."

"But how could they do that?" he asked.

"It doesn't matter, does it?" said Daniel. "The important thing is that they are here and will help us."

"Unbelievable," said Maston scratching the back of his head. "An army of samkits. Unbelievable! I have to think about this. I'll come to your tent later, Daniel. Maybe, just maybe," he muttered as he left.

When he finally did come, Jeanine was asleep. In the calm of the night breeze, they walked near the shore, a man, a boy, and two samkits. The general had a plan.

Bantu and Tamara left immediately afterwards, disappearing into the mountains. They would find their way into the plains where Resson's army camped without going through the valley entrance. In the morning, Lauren's men, working as silently as possible, began clearing the sealed valley entrance from their end. It was Maston who was now eager to open the way. His plan called for a surprise attack. On the third night, while Resson's army peacefully slept, they broke through.

In the chilly hours before morning, as Pern made its final turn around Bern, Lauren's entire army mounted. Daniel hugged Jeanine, who had wanted to ride with him at the head of the army. But Lauren refused to let her. The two princesses would be the last ones out of the valley. If it looked as though Resson was winning, they, and a small detachment of soldiers, would escape into the mountains. As long as Lauren was free, Resson could not declare victory.

The soldiers shivered as they created a snakelike line, two horses wide, that wound almost around the entire lake. They didn't question Maston's orders when he told them to remove their shirts. Nor did they call him insane when he told them of the help they'd receive. Only Daniel, seated on Hira at the top of the line, wore a shirt. Me would not stay behind, and Daniel's pocket was its home. The samkits were told not to attack the boy on the mahemuth and to protect him when he rode to the side. Daniel knew he was no match for any swordsman, so his part in this fight would be one of observer. Also, knowing that he would feel the pain of injured animals, he felt it wise to stay away from the battlefield.

When the sky began to lose some of its black color in the east, Maston moved into the cleared opening. Scouts had left earlier, and by now, all of Resson's guards were dead.

Hira was the first to enter the broad plain beyond the mountain. The men behind her turned to the left and right, beginning a long, straight line that faced the sleeping camp. Maston waited until the line was four deep and every second brought more soldiers into view. It was time. "Tell your samkits to start," he said.

Daniel thought to Bantu, telling him to begin. He forgot that not only could Bantu read his thoughts, but the

158

rest of the clans could also. So, on Daniel's silent signal, the final battle for Lithia began.

The sun had just begun to lighten the horizon with its glow when the samkits moved. Their first targets were the huge corrals at the edges of the camp. They were made of rope fences tied to posts sunk deeply into the ground. The horses would scatter, some heading into the wilderness, others creating havoc within the camp. Whatever path the horses took, it would be impossible for Resson's soldiers to mount a countercharge. Once the horses were away, the samkits would charge into the line of tents. They'd use the banner flying over Resson's tent as a beacon. Maston's army would also head for the pennant. The one quick way to end the war was to kill Resson. Without him, there was no war.

The penned horses began to pace nervously. The morning wind brought a new scent to their nostrils. Though they could see nothing, they felt danger.

Bantu was close now, and he relayed to Daniel what he saw. The guards stationed along the edge of the camp died instantly. They never saw the samkits creeping up behind them. They didn't even have a chance to scream. The samkits ran into corrals, and the horses became hysterical. Posts were pulled up from the ground as the horses surged against the ropes. Now it was the samkits who had to retreat. They couldn't survive the trampling hooves of the panicked animals.

Shouts were heard from the edge of the camp. Those cries were picked up by other voices and relayed into the center of the now-awakening army. When Daniel told Maston the horses were free, the general raised his sword and yelled, "For Lithia, for Lauren, for our fallen comrades. Charge!" He spurred his horse to a full gallop, and his men rushed to catch him. Horns blasted the morning air, and Resson knew he was under attack.

Men, some not even dressed, ran from their tents, holding their swords and ready for battle. But the sight of hundreds of howling samkits, tearing and clawing anyone in their reach, and lines of screaming horsemen bearing down on them, was too much for many of the farmer-soldiers. Countless numbers of them turned and fled. Defending Resson was not on their minds. Escaping the white and gray arrows of death was.

Daniel grabbed the pummel of his saddle and leaned forward. Already, the silent screams of injured or dying samkits and horses echoed in his mind. But he refused to fall down. He forced himself back up though his knuckles turned white as he squeezed the saddle.

But the battle was far from over. Many of the hardened, professional soldiers Resson had did not run away. Daniel saw men rally and form human chains with their swords pointed low toward the samkits. The samkits didn't charge those lines. They backed off and headed in other directions, killing whoever moved. By now, the front of Lauren's army had plowed into the line of men and tents. Swords clashed, but this time it was Resson's men who were pushed back. Too many of them had fled, seeking only to save their own lives.

And the samkits never let up. When they reached the edge of the camp, they turned and ran back into it. Though their numbers were small, they were vicious.

160

They crisscrossed the camp, making it seem as though there were thousands of them. Anyone wearing a shirt who was near a samkit was torn to pieces. The fear the animals caused demoralized Resson's men more than Lauren's charging soldiers. Resson's army gave way. The makeshift lines they made crumbled. They dropped their swords and ran toward Lauren's men, hoping that would save them from the samkits.

We are going to win! Daniel's mind shouted to Bantu. *You did it! You and your clans have saved Lithia from Resson. You are free! Your clans are free . . .*

He never finished. A pain, sharper than any he had felt before, entered his body. He looked down and, just above his pocket, saw the wooden shaft of an arrow. The things he saw, fighting men, running men, racing animals, all slowed down. Everything appeared to move in slow motion. He felt himself slipping off the giant mare. The ground took forever to hit his body. When it did, the pain returned.

He lay on his back and heard Hira gallop away. He had no energy to call after her or even turn his head. The sound of battle grew softer. He closed his eyes. Before darkness could overcome him, someone kicked him in his side. When he didn't respond, the kick came again. Daniel opened his eyes. Resson was standing in front of him.

"You did this!" he said. "You and that cursed power of yours. Well, I have repaid you."

Resson began to sway. Daniel couldn't focus his eyes so he decided to close them.

"Not yet, boy!" cried Resson, kicking him again. "I

want you to know what will happen. Then, you can die." He looked up, viewing the battle. "Lauren has won, for now. I will surrender and beg forgiveness. I will say that I truly believed her guilty. She won't kill me, for I am of royal blood. I will wait, and in five or ten years, I will strike again. Only next time, I'll make sure the job isn't bungled." He laughed at Daniel. "You haven't defeated me, boy. You have only delayed me. Now, you can die."

Daniel watched Resson drop his bow and reach for his sword. He saw the blade being raised high into the air and begin a slow arc downward that would end at his head. Something blocked his vision. Me's head. The wyerin had been trapped in his pocket by the arrow, and Daniel hadn't felt it trying to escape. Now, Me was free. From its mouth flew the sweet-smelling purple poison. Two small balls of liquid shot up. The first hit Resson on the hand that held the sword. The second hit him just below the chin.

The scream that poured from Resson's mouth was silent. The poison had already eaten into his neck and dissolved his vocal cords. Air meant for his lungs left through the widening hole in his throat. On and on the silent cry went as Resson expanded his chest trying to breathe. The sword fell harmlessly beyond Daniel's body, and when Resson brought his hand to his eyes, he saw the flesh dropping, exposing bare bones.

Once more Me spit. This time, it hit Resson in his eyes. Resson backed up one step and fell dead on the red ground.

Thanks, Me. I shall miss you. You were my best

friend. My very best friend. Be careful. Many feet. Many feet.

No go! No go! echoed in his mind. But Daniel closed his eyes and heard nothing but silence.

His name was being called. Over and over, higher and higher, the screams hit his ears. The plea was simple. "Open your eyes!" it begged. "Open your eyes!" He thought he recognized the voice. He remembered: Jeanine. He opened them. He saw Jeanine and Lauren, with many of her men, far in front of him.

No hurt no more! he heard, and a purple ball of death went flying into the air. He lowered his eyes. Me was sitting on his chest keeping everyone away.

"Me," he whispered, "it's all right. They are our friends, remember? They won't hurt us."

When Me heard Daniel, it went to his neck and rubbed its head against Daniel's ear. *Dan-yell,* it said.

Daniel weakly waved to Jeanine. His hand dropped back. *No spit, Me. Okay?*

No spit, Dan-yell, no spit.

Several men raced forward. Daniel felt his shirt being ripped and a cloth being placed over his chest. He looked up when a shadow crossed his face. Hira stood, head low. Daniel looked from Lauren to the mahemuth. Lauren understood, and removed Hira's saddle and bridle. *Thank you,* thought Daniel, looking up at Hira. *Now, be free!*

The mahemuth whinnied. Loud and long it sounded, and everywhere men stopped and looked up. Then the huge animal turned and trotted away.

Again, Daniel looked at Lauren, whose arm was

wrapped around a crying girl. Behind them, he saw a large number of samkits who had formed a semicircle around him. One samkit, who sat in the front of the circle with Tamara and Bantu, was the old samkit with the Z-shaped scar Daniel had seen before.

"The law I made is now being spread throughout the land," said Lauren. "These samkits are not our enemies. They are allies who have saved my kingdom. Their faith in me will never be forgotten, and as long as queens rule Lithia, they will never be harmed."

Will you leave now? Daniel thought to Tamara.

No, she answered. *We will stay with Jeanine. Bantu will bring my cubs.*

Daniel smiled and looked at Jeanine. She came to him, kneeling in the red mud. Daniel's voice was weak when he spoke. "They will stay with you. Bantu will bring their little ones. Soon, you'll have a house full of samkits. But remember your promise, little sister, no chains, no locks, no cages. Never."

"Don't die, Daniel. I need you," she cried. "I'll be good. I promise I'll be good."

A pain began to grow in Daniel's head. It raced from behind his eyes to the back of his head. As the pain moved, it grew and worsened. It felt as if his head were burning. He had felt this pain before, when the samkits had a mind-meet. He squeezed his eyes shut and tears dripped from their edges. Jeanine's cries faded.

Suddenly, a voice broke through the pain. *Goodbye, Daniel,* it said.

Daniel forced his eyes open. Everything was completely blurry. Everything except one old samkit.

Who . . . thought Daniel.

Some secrets must be kept. Thank you for your help, cub from another world. You spoke to our enemies for us, and they are our enemies no longer. At last, we have our peace.

The pain exploded inside his head and Daniel fainted.

Daniel felt numb and shivered. His mind was fuzzy, and he couldn't think straight. Why was he so cold? He opened his eyes. Everything was white. Where was he? This wasn't his room. Where was he? Slowly, he struggled to his feet. Icy wind blew against him and he stumbled. He grabbed the nearest thing, an oak tree, and held on to it to keep from falling. "What happened?" he said to himself. "Where am I?"

His clothes were soaking wet, his body trembled, but all he could do was press his cheek against the bark and hug the tree. He began to remember. He had left school and taken the short cut through the woods. He fell and was hit by lightning. "Yes," he said, "lightning." Then he woke up somewhere. "Where . . ." he said, "where . . ." He ignored the cold as he waited for his mind to start working. "Lithia! Jeanine!" he yelled. His head snapped around, looking in all four directions. "That's impossible," he whispered. "It couldn't have happened. It must have been a dream."

He shivered again, long and hard. "Home. I've got to get home. But where am I?" He squinted his eyes and started walking where the trees became thinner. The wind had lost some of its force and Daniel moved steadily forward. "Smoke. Where is it coming from?"

165

Through the thick, falling snow, he saw it, a chimney. "Wait a minute! That's my house!" He ran between the last of the trees and found himself at the edge of a road. Across the street, directly opposite him, was his own house.

"That will teach me not to take short cuts."

Teach what? he heard. *Me no cut. Me no want cut. Me cold!*

"What!" yelled Daniel. He tore open his jacket and looked into his shirt pocket. Coiled up at the bottom was Me, looking just as red as the red flannel shirt he wore. "Me! That's not you. You can't be real! You can't be!"

Of course Me real. You real. Me real. Real cold. Me sleep in cold.

"How did you . . . How did I . . . It wasn't a dream! It happened!"

Me . . . tell . . . you. Me . . . no . . . go. Me sleep . . . now.

Daniel looked up. He could just make out the face of his sister peering through the curtains, staring into the flying snow.

"I don't understand this, Me," he said. "Come on, let's go home."

Me . . . . . . home.

Epilogue

Even before Daniel reached the walkway, the door to his house flew open. A small figure dressed in jeans and a sweatshirt burst out. She ran, or rather was blown, into his outstretched arms. Daniel bent down and held his sister tightly. She was crying, and her arms wrapped securely around his neck. He carried her into the house and kicked the door shut behind them.

"Mom and Dad called," she said still clutching him. "They can't come home until the storm is over and the roads are clear. Your school called twice to find out if you were home. I was scared that you . . ."

She stopped in midsentence. Daniel had put her down and was staring at her. "What's the matter?" she asked. She realized Daniel was still holding both her hands, though she was two steps away from him. He had never done that before. "Now just a minute," she said breaking away from him. "Don't think I was worried about you because I cared. It was Mom and Dad I was thinking about. That was the dumbest thing you ever did, leaving school during the blizzard. I can take care of myself, you know. I'm smarter than you are, in case you've forgotten."

"If I ever do forget, you'll remind me, right?"

"You better believe I will!" she said.

Daniel started to laugh. "I don't understand what happened to me. Maybe you will when I tell you. You haven't changed a bit. Same old Evelyn."

"What do you mean, 'changed'? I saw you this morning."

Daniel dropped his coat on the floor and sat on a hall seat. He started taking off his shoes and socks. "I'm soaked, sis. Could you get me a towel?"

"Get it yourself," she said as she turned.

"I almost died today, Evelyn. Would you please stop being obnoxious for a few minutes so we can talk?"

Evelyn stopped instantly and turned back toward him as soon as he said "died." She began to shake. "It's . . . it's cold," she whispered.

"I know," he said. "How about that towel?"

For the first time, Evelyn really looked at her dripping brother. Her eyes opened and she took a deep breath. She ran into the bathroom and came back with a large bath towel.

When she returned, Daniel had already taken his pants off. Before he used the towel, he opened it and shook it out.

"It's okay," she whispered sheepishly.

"How many garter snakes are in the tank?" he asked.

"Three."

"Are you sure?" he said again. When she nodded, he started to dry himself. "Come on, let's sit by the fire." He put a few more logs on and after rearranging them with the poker and putting the screen back over the open hearth, they sat down.

"What did you want to talk about?" she said.

"Us. Now listen, and listen carefully. From today on, there's going to be a change in the way we treat each other. First, you are smarter than I am . . ."

"You better . . ."

"Evelyn, shut up and listen. Now, to start again. You are smarter than I am. You're smarter than Mom and Dad. You're smarter than the teachers in your school. You are probably smarter than most of the people on the entire planet. And everyone, Evelyn, everyone who has ever met you knows that because you keep telling them over and over. Well, that's going to stop. You're going to stop being a spoiled brat who has only one friend in the world . . ."

As soon as Daniel said brat, Evelyn got up and opened her mouth.

"And that friend is your brother! If you don't sit down, Evelyn Taylor, I will ignore you for the rest of my life. That's not a threat, sis. That's a promise!"

Evelyn had never heard Daniel speak this way. She closed her mouth and sat back down.

"Good. In the past, you've done a lot of things just to get on my nerves . . ."

"But you did . . ."

"Shut up, I said! You've done things to get on my

169

nerves, and I've done just as many things to get back at you. There were lots of times I could have taken you along when I went somewhere but didn't. There were lots of times I should have been a better brother to you but I wasn't." By now, Daniel's voice was soft, almost whispering. "I was jealous and maybe when you were little, I didn't give you any reason to love m . . . me." He waited for an answering voice inside his head, but it never came. Me must have still been asleep. "And as soon as you realized how bright you were, and what a good set of lungs you had, you didn't give anyone a chance to love you."

"It wasn't my fault," she said.

"It was both of our faults. We both did things we shouldn't have done. Evelyn, if we don't do anything about it, we'll grow further and further apart. When you become afraid in a thunderstorm, you won't have anyone to go to. And I won't have anyone to take care of."

"Why are you telling me this now?" she asked.

"I told you. Something crazy happened to me. I realized something, something I should have told you a long time ago. Something I thought I would never get the chance to tell you."

"What?"

"I love you, sis. You may be a brat. But at least you're my brat."

"You mean it? You're not just playing with me because I was worried about you?"

"I mean it."

"Me? Your sister? Evelyn? You're not teasing me?"

170

Now he laughed. "Yes, you, my sister, Evelyn."

Evelyn moved closer and wrapped her arms around him.

Telling her he cared wasn't as hard as he expected it would be, thought Daniel as he hugged her back. Before he let her go, he thought about someone else. He hoped Jeanine knew he loved her, too. He knew that he would always be there for Evelyn, and he was glad Tamara and Bantu would always be there for Jeanine. He would miss them all.

"Evelyn," he said. "I'm going to tell you what happened. But it's our secret. No one, not even Mom and Dad, can ever, ever know. Promise?"

When Evelyn pulled away, her eyes were red. "Okay," she said. "I promise. But before you tell me, I've got to tell you something. I lied to you. But I won't do it anymore, Daniel, I promise I won't."

He kept his hands on her shoulders as he looked into her face. He believed her. "Go ahead, sis," he said.

"There are only two snakes in the tank!"